YOU CAN RUN,
BUT YOU CAN'T HIDE . . .

The commander of the Soviet BMP was neither a coward nor a fool, but he did not realize what he had encountered. He tried to keep the pursuing Bradley at a distance, but Prentice pressed forward, looking for an open shot, while rounds from the BMP blasted tree trunks and branches all around him.

At last, the Soviet commander realized that he could run but he couldn't hide. He wheeled his crippled BMP and laid his gun for a desperation shot at the relentless Bradley on his tail.

The heavy stutter of the Phalanx's recoil was thrumming through the Bradley as it broke into the open, pouring a stream of fire. The Soviet crew never got off a round. The continuous skein of 37mm slugs split their lightly armored APC from glacis to exhaust grille, and the explosion of its ammunition magazine peeled back the halves like a rotted, ruptured fruit . . .

TANKWAR III:
FIRESTORM

TANKWAR III: FIRESTORM

LARRY STEELBAUGH

BERKLEY BOOKS, NEW YORK

TANKWAR III: FIRESTORM

A Berkley Book / published by arrangement with
the author

PRINTING HISTORY
Berkley edition / July 1991

ISBN: 0-425-12819-9

A BERKLEY BOOK ® TM 757,375
Berkley Books are published by The Berkley Publishing Group,
200 Madison Avenue, New York, New York 10016.
The name "Berkley" and the "B" logo
are trademarks belonging to Berkley Publishing Corporation.

PRINTED IN THE UNITED STATES OF AMERICA

10 9 8 7 6 5 4 3 2 1

This book is dedicated to the indomitable spirit of all prisoners of conscience everywhere.

1

The first day of the sole battlefield nuclear exchange of World War III, in the area of southern Germany known to NATO as SOUTHAG, was the worst for Max Tag. When he saw the distant, intense expansions of light in the predawn sky and felt the very air around him gel and shudder with the dying ripples of atomic aftershocks, he had his first doubt ever—and it ran bone deep—about the importance of being a soldier, even the necessity. He could not deny an overwhelming sense of insignificance when faced by the awful and awesome power released through fission from a lump of uranium no larger than a fifty-caliber slug. Even at this distance—eighty kilometers from the initial impacts but less than thirty from the disguised line of Soviet launchers that, Tag was certain, would be the targets of Allied counter-battery fire—the concussions were more felt than heard. They filled him with greater terror and helplessness than he had experienced while surviving that rain of two-thousand-pound bombs from a B-52 in Honduras. Anyone who has not witnessed the effects of nuclear blasts has no frame of reference for imaging them.

A commander's duty saved Tag from the numbness of despair. While there were still his men who crewed the XM-F4 tank No Slack Too, the half-dozen remaining Jagd Kommandos, N. Sain and his sidemen-cum-keepers, as well as the surviving clerks and drivers of Lieutenant Prentice's "ranger" platoon to consider, he could not indulge himself in reflection or self-pity. They needed him to be a rock, and so he was a rock.

"N. Sain," Tag said, his voice loud and steady, "scrounge."

The renegade reservist batted his stoned-angelic eyes.

The last of the raiders had stumbled out of the cavern, awakened by N. Sain's playing the Jimi Hendrix version of "The Star-Spangled Banner," in homage to the nuclear dawn. Tag turned to them, his back to N. Sain's shrapnel-scoured Bradley.

"Everyone," he said. He swung his arm to include the naked acres of mine tailings that fronted the worked face of the mountain, as well as the surrounding woods, where the buckled carcasses of Soviet BRMs and light armor still lay smoldering from yesterday's ambush and battle. "Get anything you think we can use—food, fuel, ammo, medical supplies, radios, the works. Load what you can in the Bradley. Move now. Fast."

Tag turned to Lieutenant Giesla Ruther—his comrade, lover, and with the death of her brother, Tag's friend Heinrich Holz, now commander of the Jagd Kommando detachment—and said, "Gies, use your gun buggies and drag us some timbers and sheet iron and whatever else you can find out of the old shafts—anything we can use to seal off the gallery, make it atom proof."

Sergeant Dunn, the demolition-man-turned-squad-leader, dropped back from the men scattering toward the blasted Soviet vehicles and said, "Hey, Captain, that's a piece a cake. I can drop enough ceiling in those shafts, won't nothing leak through."

"Okay," said Tag, "you've got the job." He turned back to Giesla.

"Gies, go ahead and get us enough material to make a barricade for the main shaft. And something for sandbags, if you can find anything."

Giesla nodded and went inside the shaft, calling to her Jagd Kommandos as she went.

Tag had Wheels Latta, the driver of the No Slack Too, bring the tank outside and park it near the mouth of the tunnel. He put the XM-F4 on full NBC (nuclear, biological, and chemical) alert to monitor for any stray radiation or other toxins. He prayed that the weather held out of the north-northeast and delivered on its promise of rain.

Fruits Tutti, the electronics whiz kid who was the loader on the No Slack Too, set a mast antenna and a remote-controlled mini-dish high on the slope above the mine face and ran coaxial cable back down to the cavern. If they couldn't move or shoot, Tag thought, they would at least leave all their communication options open. But for the time being, the electromagnetic storms of atomic particles from the distant blasts had masked radio traffic in a blizzard of static and squeezed the satellite horizon to ninety degrees, above them and to the east, and closing fast.

Tag sat in his commander's chair, eyeing the NBC monitors and popping into a cold sweat each time the radiation counter spiked from wayward neutrinos that would pass through the earth itself on their single-minded way to infinity. But the ambient radiation level remained below that of a hospital X-ray room.

By dawn, an hour later, Dunn had his strings of charges set, and the men and vehicles had all assembled outside. In addition to whatever was in the Bradley and in the gun buggies that had fanned out to help with the scrounging, Tag saw ranks and files of gasoline and water cans, ricks of crated rations and ammunition, piles of weapons, medical supplies, NBC protective uniforms, gas masks, radios, maps, code books, and several dozen half-liter bottles of vodka. The men had even recovered the towed fuel tank that N. Sain had taken in their first battle together in the Danube valley. It sat behind the cosmic killer's scourged Bradley, filled with siphoned diesel.

Tag tried not to think of how many Communist nuclear devices might be annealed to the melted armor of the Soviet BRMs that littered the mountain around him, or even lying exposed in ruptured containers. Four of Prentice's Rangers came up carrying two dull metal cylinders, each covered in stenciled Cyrillics and bearing the international trefoil symbol for radioactive material.

"Captain Max," said one of the men, grunting as he eased his end of the cylinder to the ground, "whadda we get for capturing a Commie A-bomb? Two of 'em, in fact."

"Yeah," said another, stepping back to admire the canisters as though they were trophy trout, "what kinda medals we get for this, sir?"

Tag's reaction was torn between knowing the intelligence value of the warheads and feeling a cold roil in his belly at the thought of having the things nearby. Hell, they were safer than the ones still scattered in the BRMs. Still . . .

"Medal, my ass," Tag said. "Summary court-martial is more like it. All of you fuckers are restricted."

Dunn cranked his hell-box detonator and dropped sheets of rock from the ceilings of the next-to-last access shaft and the main work shaft, sealing them as neatly as deadfalls in the tomb of a Pharaoh.

There was no waiting for the dust to settle. As soon as Dunn had accounted for all his charges, the men and machines began moving the Soviet materiel inside, wrapping their faces in wet rags against the choking clouds of rock dust. Once everything was safely in the cavern, Tag let the men eat breakfast outside. It was a beautiful sunrise, streaked by purple mare's-tail clouds.

At midmorning, a group of the partisans from a nearby village arrived with some of their families, the veterinarian and staff from the animal research hospital where Tag's wounded had been treated, and four large, impassive Alsatian dogs. They swelled the population of the abandoned mine to more than eighty, but they also brought welcome foodstuffs—real food—and the courage of community, a sense of civilization. The local people set to work with a brisk efficiency to make themselves at home. They took over the menial chores of cooking and organizing the "household" — everything from locating latrines to adjusting the trim on the white-gas lanterns to keep them from smoking their globes.

With the soldiers freed to inventory and disburse the Soviet gear, while the creature comforts were being seen to by the civilians, a comfortable pattern of rapt distraction fell into place. Each man and woman tried to become absorbed in the tasks at hand and to pretend to a companionable silence. No one spoke of what had begun; none had any words for it. They became like the family of someone dying of AIDS, trying to consider it without saying the word. N. Sain and his retrorock sidemen, Mad Dog and Rabies, alone seemed invigorated, not enervated by the pall of fission that hung over the war.

Tag had allowed N. Sain to continue broadcasting some rhythmic, blues-based tunes over his Bradley's loudspeaker, with the volume at what N. Sain scorned as "elevator decibels." But after twenty continuous hours of decisions and command, Tag found himself becoming manic with exhaustion. He ordered himself to get some sleep and was in no mood for the mystopoeic maunderings of N. Sain, who snagged Tag like the Ancient Mariner when he passed the Bradley, headed for his own tank.

"Captain Maximus," N. Sain crooned, his eyes glinting like isinglass in the lantern-cast shadows of the mine, "we are there, Avatar of Ambush. We have seen the Eve of Destruction. This is really it: the fire this time. Fear-fucking juggernaut ablaze on the slope to consummation, perfect intercourse with the Dark Divinity, the democracy of death. We'll shuffle off this mortal coil all the way to Buffalo and be one with nature's unyielding force. We will *be* the center of the sun, man. Too fucking much."

"N. Sain," Tag said wearily, "for once, I really, really hope you are wrong."

The paladin of rock and roll stood pop-eyed, bemused by Tag not replying in his usual parody of mystical effusion, and watched the haggard tanker plod heavily across the gritty floor of the cavern toward the No Slack Too.

Wheels, Fruits, and Ham Jefferson—the exhausted crew of the No Slack Too—were sprawled on their inflatable bedrolls. Tag dragged his own sleeping bag out of the gear locker and unrolled it on the side of the tank away from his crew, just wanting a brief illusion of solitude. He worked the foot pump built into one corner of the bag and inflated the mattress. Tired as he was, he could not control the tumble of thoughts that raced through his mind. And they brought him nothing but frustration and futility.

For the moment, they were treed, unable to run or fight. The war and the weapons of that war had overwhelmed him, outstripped his resources and his ability to be a significant factor in the fight. The horrible feeling that had soured in him at the nuclear dawn's first light returned now. But one insistent voice in the chatter of possibilities that ran through his mind told him to be calm, that matters would have to resolve themselves without his help. They were all still alive, probably not within any targeted strike zone, upwind of the main battlefronts, and well protected in the granite womb of the mine. He had done all he could—but it was not enough. Tag ground his teeth and thought of taking a sleeping pill. He knew he would be less than he needed to be if he did not get some sleep, but he was equally leery of being in a drug stupor if something did come down.

Giesla rescued him from the horns of his dilemma. With her hair down and wearing her helmet, she looked ever the Valkyrie as she came to him out of the gloom of the hushed cavern, emerging slowly in his vision like a photographic print in a developing tray. The sight of her focused his thoughts.

In the few seconds that it took her to reach the foot of his bedroll, Tag remembered everything he knew and felt about her and, marveling, was touched by her courage. She had not even been distracted from her duty by grief over her brother's death—neither of them had—and that sense of loss was part of what he felt for her now, how it had been sublimated into a fighting fury that had spelled ruin for the Soviet column trying to move nukes to the front and how deep had been that loss to create such ferocity in her.

Giesla stopped at the end of Tag's sleeping bag and said, "Good. I am glad you are getting some rest, Max."

Tag rolled his head and put on a stiff grin. "Going through the drill, at least," he said.

"I was monitoring your radio earlier," said Giesla, "but nothing is clear. There was a lot of aircraft traffic, however, from both sides. Nothing from your command?"

Tag shook his head and massaged the back of his neck. "There's so much electromagnetic bullshit flying around that even the satellite pictures were breaking up. All I could see was this goddamn monster hot-spot. I'm just praying now that the weather holds out of the north and, well . . ." He let the sentence die.

"And what?"

"And that they don't start dropping the big ones." There was no humor in his grin. "Hell, for all we know, they may have already started. Either way, I'm afraid our war is over, Gies."

Giesla stepped around the sleeping bag and embraced Tag. She wanted to tell him how much she loved him, admired him, how brave he was, how resourceful, but instead she felt the tension in his neck and shoulders and said, "Lie down, Max, and let me work some of this out of you."

Tag peeled off his jumpsuit and stretched facedown on the inflated ribs of his bedroll, feeling them roll beneath him. Giesla straddled his hips with her long, muscular legs and began massaging his back, shoulders, and neck with long strokes of the heels of her hands. His muscles resisted at first, but at last she felt them relax beneath her touch.

"You have done well, Max," she said.

"Umm," he mumbled. "Can't do much better than to be alive in this deal."

Giesla squeezed Tag's wide, flat latissimus dorsi. "No," she said, "I mean here, Max. This place could have been a panic. You say we are out of the war, but you kept everyone in it, in their minds, and that has kept their courage up. No one here has quit. That is what I mean, Max." She bent forward and kissed the furrow of a scar on his shoulder blade.

Tag squirmed against the shifting tubes of his mattress, and Giesla let him turn over. She sat across his hips, facing him, back erect and arms akimbo.

"Giesla," said Tag, "you give me too much credit and everybody else too little, including yourself. I'd say we all did our jobs. Hell, did you see MD and Rabies helping that old hausfrau set up her cot?"

Giesla smiled and leaned forward, bracing her palms on Tag's chest as she lowered her face to within an inch of his. "Yes," she said. "They provided me with private quarters as well." She ran the sharp tip of her tongue between her teeth. "Perhaps you should inspect them?"

Tag allowed that, as he was her commander and therefore responsible for her billet, he should.

They carried his bedroll to Giesla's cubicle, arranged in part within an excavated niche, where they made love sotto voce, stifling the sounds of their pleasure and grief and desperate, desperate hope.

Their second day in the theater of nuclear war was not as bad as the first, but it did not begin that way.

After spending an hour with Giesla, much of it in silent embrace, Tag dragged his bedroll back to the No Slack Too and slept soundly for more than five hours. He awoke to trembling stone and the maddened howls of animals.

At first his dream took opportunity with the shock waves moving through the earth and turned them to the tossing of a boat on a rolling sea. Even the howls, for a moment, were the wind, and it was the violence of that wind that woke him.

"Incoming!" a voice screamed—and Tag realized it was his own. He whipped away the twisted halves of his sleeping bag and scrambled to his knees, searching the shadows for a source of the howling. The German shepherds—of course.

Backlit by a lantern on the other side of the tank, Ham Jefferson came to Tag's side and knelt by the fender.

"It's happening again, Bossman," said the long-faced black gunner. "They hittin' the launchers we spotted."

Tag's lips smacked dryly as he tried to engage something in his swelter of thoughts and morning terrors.

"Fruits has got the radiation counter wired through the mini-dish, Boss," Ham continued, "and our hand-held is set up in the shaft by the barricade. But we got nothing so far. Any drill?"

Tag came to grips with consciousness and said, "Somebody shut up those goddamn dogs." But they had already been calmed to a whimper by the young twin girls who usually tended them in their kennels.

Ham cocked his head quizzically, and Tag added, "Then let's get some chow and square this joint away. After that, I'll want after-action reports from everybody, including a complete sitrep on the No Slack Too. That should keep you yahoos out of mischief until lunchtime, and I'll have thought of something else by then."

Ham grinned and stood up. "You know, Boss-man," he said, "I think garrison life is turning you into an asshole."

"Jefferson," said Tag, also rising heavily to his feet, "consider your jive ass court-martialed. Now, go find me some coffee, and you'll get mercy; otherwise, it's justice."

The nuclear barrage was over in minutes, leaving an eerie stillness in the cavern that left Tag abashed at his shouted warning. But no one mentioned his cry coming out of sleep, so he didn't bring it up. During the rest of the morning, under the light of more lanterns than were really needed, except for the comfort they provided, the community of raiders and partisans and noncombatants ate and tended to their duties with a steadily abating sense of dread. Tag spent part of his time passing among them, with Giesla to translate when needed, talking to small groups and individuals, telling them as much as he knew and at least some of what they wanted to hear—a confident voice.

After lunch, Tag called a meeting of the officers and NCOs and the senior partisans, more for the rhythm of normalcy than for any tactical or administrative end. Lieutenant Prentice had a report on his wounded and effectives, and Giesla gave a brisk inventory of their captured supplies. Fruits Tutti reported a slight but steady rise in the ambient radiation level outside, one he described as "like bein' in a room fulla radium watches," but nothing so far had leaked through the six-foot-thick barricade of timbers, stone, steel, and sandbags sealing the main shaft.

With that said, Tag saw the only thing left to do was go outside and check on the weather, using the sandbagged crawlspace that the raiders had engineered into the barricade in the shaft. He quickly vetoed any volunteers going along.

"No," he said with finality to an insistent Prentice. "Just get me a radio to use, Chuck, while I go suit up."

The NBC protective uniforms that Tag and his men had been issued in Brussels along with the XM-F4 came in bundles of ten, one bundle per man. They were whole-body coveralls made of a filmy gray synthetic, with a clear plastic visor and microns-thin breathing filters built in and a cumulative-radiation/toxin patch on the sleeve. Each came packed in a lead-foil envelope about the size of a glossy magazine, which could also be used for disposing of the contaminated suit.

"Yeah, and save your friggin' gum wrappers," Fruits Tutti whined as he zip-locked the triple seams up the back of Tag's suit.

"What's it like out there now, Fruits?" Tag asked, his voice sounding distant beneath the impermeable skin. He shook out the arms and legs of the suit and, glancing over one shoulder, stepped back into the radio harness Fruits Tutti was holding.

"Nothing to it, Cap," the loader replied. "Ya don't even need sunglasses out there. Probably get more RADs offa the radar screen." He settled the radio straps across Tag's shoulders, plugged in the jack from a CVC, and handed it to him.

"Thanks," Tag said. He pulled the Kevlar VI helmet gingerly over his suited head, being careful not to pinch the fabric, cinched it with the chin strap, and picked up the hand-held radiation/toxin detector beside him on the floor of the cavern.

"Okay," he said, stepping forward as awkwardly as a novice moon walker, "let's tear it up."

Prentice's men had cleared the crawl space at the top of the barricade, except for two ammo boxes full of dirt and rock that were the final plug. When they were hauled free, Tag could feel a current of air against his protective suit, and one of the GIs said, "Yeah, that's rain I smell."

Tag mounted the ammo boxes cautiously and inched across the top of the barricade. The light from the mouth of the shaft that lay beyond a single gentle bend was milky and diffuse. Tag lowered himself crabwise down the barricade and activated the radio switch in his CVC.

"Butcher Boy Charlie, this is Butcher Boy Actual. How do you read me? Over."

"Butcher Boy, this is Charlie," Fruits Tutti responded. "It'll be better oncet you're outside. The whip on the hill will get ya then. Over."

"Roger, Charlie," Tag said, grinning largely. "Out." He promised himself that when they all got out of this, he was personally going to pay for Fruits Tutti's diction lessons.

Wind whipped the loose protective suit against Tag's chest and legs as he stepped from the mouth of the shaft. The sky was low, gray, and fast, with tendrils like smoke trailing from the molten-slag bottoms of the clouds. It was holding out of the north-northeast. He knew that if he pulled the tab from the gas-mask port on the suit, he could breathe fall air that smelled of rain. But denying himself that was less irksome than being deprived of his hearing. Beneath the poreless skin of the suit and the close-fitting CVC, he was practically deaf to everything but the radio and the high wind.

He swept 180 degrees with the radiation counter and found what Fruits said was true: the ambient level was about what a family used to get by watching old-fashioned cathode-ray tube TV.

"Charlie, this is Butcher Boy. Over."

"Charlie. Over."

"Charlie, I'm going to run a few radiation readings, then check our toys up on the ridge and look for any sign of movement. You copy? Over."

"Roger that, Butcher Boy," Fruits said. "I copy. Over."

"Butcher Boy out."

Tag walked a wide arc from the mouth of the mine shaft, across the waste of tailings with its ruins of machinery and Soviet armor, along the edge of the forest, and back to the place from which he and the No Slack Too had last fought, in the forest beyond the mined face of the mountain. The shifting buffets of wind tore at his filmy NBC suit, plastering it to him like Saran Wrap, but the sound of the wind was only a distant soughing beneath his CVC. His radiation counter did not pick up anything to indicate leaks from whatever Soviet nukes might be left in the shattered convoy.

The suit was sweltering now and chafing the nape of his neck as Tag lowered his head and started up the slope to the bench land above the mine, where Fruits had located their antennas. He followed the coaxial cable, never looking up to see how far he had to go until the grade began to flatten and the readout on his counter took a dive back toward zero.

Tag peered through the slightly fogged visor of the NBC suit and saw the antenna array in a bowl-shaped depression where a giant larch had once grown, its decomposed remains now lying like shadow on the forest floor. Tag swept the area again with his counter, and still the ambient radiation level was well within safe parameters. He shrugged and thought and said aloud, "Ah, hell. Why not?"

With that, Tag sat on the edge of the bowl-shaped hollow and unfastened the three layers of zip locks that ran like a razor slash from ear to ear beneath the visor of the NBC suit. He turned up the volume on the CVC radio link and put the helmet on the ground beside him, then peeled the headpiece of the suit back off over his brow. The wind hit his sweaty skin like a blast from a meat locker, and the whole thrashing of the forest came rushing in his ears. It was like coming up from underwater.

Tag's heart beat fast. The growing storm, while not yet violent, was sublime in its intensity,

sending half-formed funnels swirling across the
bottom of the cloud mass and whipping the tree
trunks in a dervish dance to the syncopated beat
of surrounding thunder. Hardwoods had turned
up the pale undersides of their leaves, and needles on the larch and fir blew straight out from
the branches. Tag knew the tradition of storms
over the battlefield, the myth of Napoleon's own
cannon causing the downpour at Waterloo, and
he could not keep from wondering whether this
storm was in fact one of those, adding another
meaning to "nuclear precipitation." If it was, and
if it held its course, it was also their salvation,
blowing the fallout downrange and, when the
rain finally came, settling the scatter of radioactive dust.

The effects of these thoughts and the action of
the storm worked like a tonic on Tag's anxiety
for the safety of his command. The storm itself
was invigorating, and he sat for several minutes
simply enjoying the sensation, trying to fill himself with its exhilaration. A twinge of guilt finally
spoiled his reverie. He picked up the CVC, settled it on his head, and called in, "Charlie, this
is Butcher Boy Actual. Have reached communications array. All is strack; no sign of movement.
Over."

"Roger, Butcher Boy," Fruits Tutti responded.
"So whadda ya telling me for? Over."

"Charlie, this is Actual; fuck you too very much.
Out."

Tag eased the CVC off and reached behind his
head to pull the headpiece of his NBC suit back
into position. He hooked the throat vent with
his thumbs—and froze. Even through the rush
of wind and the rattling of branches, he heard a

sound that didn't belong to the forest, the sound of diesel motors.

Tag snatched up his helmet under one arm and rolled into the depression next to the antennas. He lay still and listened carefully, conscious not to be distracted by his own breathing. All he could catch were scraps of sound torn by the wind and coming from who-knew-where, but coming closer. Tag eased back beneath the lip of the bowl and slipped the helmet back on.

"Charlie, this is Actual. Have motorized movement. No visual contact. Am abandoning radio with transmit link open to recon for movement. Do you copy? Over."

"Roger, Actual. Charlie copy. Over."

"Charlie, pass the word: prepare to move. Actual out."

Tag unstrapped the radio and refastened the headpiece of his suit. He didn't like leaving the radio, but he couldn't hear with it on, and it was too awkward carrying both the CVC and the radiation counter in his hands. What he really wanted to abandon was the NBC suit. He tugged it away from his armpits and crotch, where sweat and condensation had glued it to his body, picked up the radiation counter, and slithered over the rim of the bowl.

Scuttling at a high crawl, stopping to listen and scan with the radiation detector, Tag moved rapidly through the trees, homing on instinct and the shreds of diesel sounds until he locked in on a noise moving parallel to the axis of the ridge somewhere above him. When he turned toward it and pointed the snout of his radiation counter up slope, the digital display on the instrument flashed a spike, recalibrated itself, and showed a source emitting

ten-fold normal radiation. Tag reflexively touched
the zip-lock seams of his suit.

With one eye on the counter and the other on the
storm-buffeted mountainside, Tag crept toward
the noise. He had not traveled a hundred meters
before he knew that it was more than one vehicle
making the sound. In another hundred meters, he
could not distinguish a single motor from the wall
of clanking and snarling commotion.

At last he saw movement and dived for the cover
of a stand of small fir, their lowest branches only
inches off the ground. Cursing the light color of
the NBC suit, Tag parted the fir needles and kept
his head back in the shadow. Twenty-five meters
from him a confused column of Communist vehicles was making its best speed through the forest,
ignoring discipline and its order of march as vehicles juked among the trees and forged ahead at
every opportunity. There were T-80 and T-64B
tanks, BMPs, BRMs, open trucks with swarms
of soldiers in the back, and light four-wheel
ambulances passing all the rest. These, Tag realized, were the survivors of that morning's Allied
nuclear strike against the Soviet launchers, the
false line designed to lure the Allies into massing
for a ground assault, concentrating targets for the
Communist nukes.

Tag watched for a half hour, counting more than
a hundred vehicles, many of them clearly meat
wagons, loaded with Warsaw Pact dead, all of them
dosed with high levels of atomic radiation. It was
a sort of satisfaction for Tag, a grim and hollow
victory.

He flinched from a resounding clap of thunder,
which was followed at once by the first sheet of
driving rain that swept across the mountainside,

rattling through the leaves like hail on a tin roof and stinging Tag's neck and arms through the thin suit. When the next wave hit, he scrambled out of his cover and back down slope to his radio.

Settling the CVC on his head, Tag made a quick report to Fruits and started back for the cavern, pounded by the rain that beaded and streaked on his visor.

Just inside the mouth of the mine shaft, Tag peeled away the headpiece from his suit, shook himself off, and ran the radiation/toxin detector over the cumulative-dose patch on his sleeve, causing hardly a blip on the oscillascreen. Tag replaced his helmet and, out of a tanker's habit, touched the side of the CVC before radioing to Fruits, "Charlie, this is Actual. I'm clean and coming in. Make a hole. Over."

"Well, come on, den," Fruits said at Tag's elbow, causing him to start.

"What the hell are you doing here, Tutti?" Tag demanded.

"Hey, Cap," Fruits said, throwing his hands in front of him as he backed away, "you said to be ready to roll, and we're ready."

Tag shucked the CVC and said, "Well, this is still the Army, Fruits, so let's get unready. We're right where we need to be for now. C'mon, and I'll give everybody the skinny."

As the waves of rain and wind slashed across the Jura, Tag and his loader moved down the shaft toward the cavern, past the disassembled barricade, and into the gallery, where the raiders and the civilians stood awaiting the order to move.

"Okay, everybody," Tag said, "stand down. Officers and NCOs come with me."

Tag rallied his command group around the No Slack Too and delivered a short briefing on what he had seen.

"So," he concluded, "until we can get some word from Command—and I hope that's in the next twenty-four hours—our best move is no move at all. Right now, things are breaking our way."

He looked at Lieutenant Prentice and said, "Chuck, get two of your men in NBCs out in the shaft as a listening post. We do have those Ivans in the area, and probably some strays. As long as the weather is with us, there's no need to stay bottled up, so we'll leave the barricade down. Blackout curtains only. Any questions?"

"Hey, Boss," Ham Jefferson called from the turret of the XM-F4, where he was monitoring the radio, "we just got a burp on the ComNet."

"Decoded?" Tag asked.

"It's in the computer now," the gunner said.

By the time Tag had mounted the rear deck of his tank, Ham had a fresh printout ready for him. He studied the single page, thick with eight-point type, for several minutes, oblivious to the tension building in the silence.

Tag looked up from the message poker-faced and surveyed those around him impassively for a moment, before breaking into a wide grin.

"People," he said with mock gravity, "we have to get ready for company. We have some guests arriving tomorrow at first light from the U.S.- by-God-Army."

A whoop of joy went off like flash powder in the cavern. But Tag had not read them all of the message.

2

After midnight the wind fell and the storm settled into a hard, soaking rain that lifted two hours before dawn. Tag awoke when it quit, coming up from a good deep sleep in his commander's chair, where he had dozed off to the rhythm of the rain on the hatch, after he had moved the tank outside to await the airborne.

Tag sent his crew back into the cavern one by one, to fetch coffee and hit the latrine, then sounded reveille and had his mixed mob of raiders, partisans, and noncombatants standing to when confirmation of the Allied assault came over the radio, in the clear and in real time.

Minutes later, as Tag stood outside the No Slack Too talking to Giesla, Wheels popped through his hatch and said, "Cap'n, we got LandSat, and I think you oughta come take a look."

Tag dropped into his fighting seat and called up his VLD—very large display—screen, a 40cm X 40cm high-resolution monitor that projected a liquid-crystal image translated from the satellite data on any grid from 100 meters to 300 kilometers, at magnifications to distinguish objects as small as the household cat. Calling up a scale that would first give him a panorama of their sector, Tag instructed the computer to

overlay the visual and radar images to provide
him an enhanced composite of SOUTHAG.

With Wheels monitoring his own screen, and
Ham and Fruits crowding each other for a view
from the turret, Tag scanned the VLD and inhaled
a thin whistle. He didn't need to explain the
images to his crew; they could all see clearly
the comma-shaped stain of atomic devastation
that the Allied counterstrikes had spread across
SOUTHAG. The head of the comma, between
Lake Constance and the Danube valley, marked
the heaviest Soviet troop concentrations, and
the tail followed the false front of launch sites
stretching across the Jura. A scattering of hot spots
roughly parallel to the inside curve of the comma
plotted the Communist strikes against NATO
positions. Even within the blot of the comma,
however, the area was not blanketed. There were
corridors among the ground-zero points where a
tank less sophisticated than the No Slack Too,
with its array of NBC defenses, could operate
without serious concern for radiation. And there
was no way yet to reckon how many of the Soviets had survived in the mountain defiles to the
south. Tag's spirits rose: perhaps his war was
not quite over.

The first heavy drone of C-130s passed overhead
at 0530. At 0550, following the third wave of aircraft, a stick of jumpers unfurled their canopies
above a half-dozen descending cargo chutes and
dropped in parallel columns across the waste of
mine tailings, then another and another, until a
full reinforced company of Rangers were on the
ground twenty miles behind what yesterday had
been the Soviet line. The worst casualties were a
few sprained ankles from landing in the rocks.

Tag stood in his hatch, watching as the Rangers collected their chutes and fell to breaking open the cargo containers, when an impossibly tall figure unfolded like a carpenter's rule from the billows of a collapsed shroud, shed his harness, and ambled away from the assembling company in the direction of the No Slack Too.

It took a moment before Tag recognized him as Colonel Barlow, the black officer on General Ross Kettle's staff who had briefed them in Brussels when they had been placed under direct command of Kettle himself— SACEUR, the Supreme Allied Commander in Europe.

Barlow spotted Tag in the hatch of the No Slack Too and raised his head in greeting, saying, as casually as if they were meeting at the officer's club, "Oh, hello. There you are, Captain." He shrugged off his field-transport pack and let it slip to the ground.

"Colonel Barlow," said Tag, as he hoisted himself from the hatch and slid over the glacis of the XM-F4. His boots crunched on the rock, and he stepped forward to take Barlow's outstretched hand. "This is quite a surprise."

"Well," said Barlow in a Tidewater drawl, "since you came to visit us last time, the general thought we wouldn't bother you again."

"Yeah," said Tag, "that steak and cold beer would be hard to take again so soon."

Barlow dropped Tag's hand and craned his neck forward. "I'm glad you feel that way, captain," he said. "The truth is, the only reason I'm here is to make sure that your orders cannot possibly be compromised. They are verbal, from SACEUR, for your ears only."

Barlow let that sink in, and Tag nodded silently.

"Obviously," Barlow continued, "you received our earlier message." Tag nodded again. "And I presume you have some idea about the battlefield dispositions from your satellite data. If you like, I can fill you in on the big picture before we get down to the details of your mission."

"Okay," Tag said, "I'd like. Can we let my other officers and senior NCOs in on it, too?"

"Of course," Barlow said. He nudged his pack with one foot. "They'll want their mail, anyway."

At that moment, a spasm of small-arms fire convulsed in the forest and quickly settled in to a steady tattoo. Ricochets whined everywhere, and Rangers and raiders and partisans all dived for cover, forming a perimeter as they did. Barlow picked up his pack and stepped casually into the lee of the No Slack Too.

"Well, well," he said, "it looks as though we were right."

"About what?" Tag asked as he eyed the wood-line.

"We suspected that, with all the nuclear devices scattered around your positions here, the Soviets might try to send in sappers to detonate them. That's why all the Rangers."

Tag looked back and grinned at Barlow. "Well, then, Colonel," he said, "how about a little ride?"

"A pleasure, captain."

Tag took his position at the mini-gun on the turret and let the colonel fold himself into the commander's seat.

"Wheels," Tag called over the intercom, "to the sound of the guns, my man. Fruits, take the Phalanx, and Ham, keep an HE in the tube and a beehive on the carousel. Move."

Spitting rocks from its treads, the XM-F4 rose

on its air-torsion suspension and sprang toward
the firefight in the trees.

"Swing wide," Tag ordered. "Let's go for the
flank."

Wheels dodged around the burned hulks of two
BMPs, hit the woods, and began a series of wild
switchbacks through the maze of fissures south
of their redoubt, following the map he had made
in his mind three days before. Running quiet and
fast, the No Slack Too was almost on top of one
of the Communist recon teams before Tag knew
it. He saw the corkscrew rocket smoke from an
RPG moments before the armor-piercing grenade
detonated against the glacis of his tank and sent
an ear-ringing blast of shrapnel flying harmlessly
over the face of the No Slack Too. Reacting on
instinct, Tag whipped the Gatling-barreled mini-
gun toward the source of the contrail, shouting,
"Slow-attack speed," through the intercom as he
touched the electronic trigger and swept the gout
of .223 fire after a pair of fleeing figures, lifting
both of them off their feet in a spray of blood and
flinging them lifeless to the ground. He saw more
movement at the edge of his vision.

"Targets. One o'clock," he barked, and both the
main turret and the Phalanx cupola tracked right.
"Chop 'em, Fruits."

With the sound of his own gun drowned in the
shuddering onslaught from the 37mm, Tag continued to pour fire into the Communist positions.
The depleted-uranium slugs from the Phalanx literally exploded tree trunks as Fruits scythed the
forest with the heavy gun, setting up a crashing
of timber and roll of ordnance that blotted out the
screams from the Soviet sappers whose flank they
had fallen on.

Wheels had been forced to a crawl as they moved inexorably on the Communist skirmishers while tacking through the fissures on the face of the mountain. One Communist soldier, in an act of suicidal heroism, had balled himself in a niche of one crevasse and played dead as the No Slack Too straddled his ditch with its treads and passed overhead. He stood when the XM-F4 cleared him and pulled the pin from an RGO fragmentation grenade, thinking to dart forward and wedge it in the tracks of the tank, when he saw Tag standing in the hatch and made a split-second decision to go for the man instead of the machine. He heaved the grenade in a high arc toward the man in the hatch and unslung his AK-74.

With the Phalanx and Wheels's 7.62mm and now Barlow bringing the commander's coaxial machine gun into play, Tag had silenced the minigun and was pivoting it from flank to flank, in case there were any stay-behinds. The movement in the periphery of his vision registered too late for him to swing the gun mount to meet it. Reflexively, his left hand shot out like a shortstop nailing a line drive. The moment his flesh made contact with the serrated grenade, Tag knew what it was. He threw from his shoulder, never bending his arm, catapulting the grenade back along its incoming trajectory. At the same instant, a burst of fire from the sapper's AK sang off the turret, one round searing a furrow beneath Tag's armpit and another striking the crown of his Kevlar VI helmet, twisting it nearly sideways. He ducked down in the turret, fighting to right the CVC, when the grenade he had repelled exploded just feet from the rear of the No Slack Too. A piece of hot shrapnel caromed off the lip of the hatch and hit him in the back of the hand.

Cursing under his breath as he pushed his head and shoulders back up through the hatch, Tag saw the Communist trooper, his legs flayed by the explosion, still trying to shoulder his rifle and pull himself into a fighting position. Tag felt tremendous admiration for the man as he whipped his Baretta 9mm from its shoulder harness and shot the sapper twice in the face.

Regaining his stance behind the mini-gun, Tag located the focus of a heavy concentration of fire from the Rangers: an abandoned BRM with its 12.7mm still operable and turned on the advancing Americans. The line-of-sight gap through the trees to the BRM was no more than a foot wide.

"Stop," Tag ordered his driver. "Ham, target. Five degrees right."

The turret moved around him, and Tag heard his gunner reply, "Confirmed."

"Shoot."

"Shot."

Tag imagined he could see the leaves and branches bend with the flight of the 120mm HE round through the seam in the trees. The impact of the cannon shot literally tore the BRM to pieces, separating all eight wheels from the chassis and all six of the sappers in and around it from all the grief that flesh is heir to.

"Splish-splash, Mister Jefferson," Tag said. The left side of his jumpsuit was warm and sticky against his ribs, and trying not to think about it had, he knew, made him a little silly. But now, with the fight over on this flank and the Rangers moving up on his right, he also knew he had to see how badly he was hit.

"Wheels," he called over the intercom, "hold this position. Fruits, get the medical kit and come up here."

Fruits was there in an instant, wriggling up through the hatch past Tag's legs, to sit on the lip across from him and help his commander peel back the sodden upper portion of his fatigues. The commander's hatch banged open, and the tall figure of Colonel Barlow climbed like a mantis up onto the turret.

Fruits had already irrigated the wound with peroxide and water and was unwrapping a pressure dressing, when Barlow crabbed up next to them.

"How bad, sergeant?" he asked.

"Ah," Fruits kvetched, working quickly and intently, "he'll do anything for attention, sir."

Barlow cocked his head at Tag quizzically.

Tag winced as Fruits applied the dressing. "It's the only way I've got to know they still love me, Colonel," he said.

A look of relief passed over Barlow's face. "Well," he said, "I'm glad that's all it is. Now let's get you back. If I let you get killed here, the general will have my ass, Captain. And *that* is not going to happen."

For a staff officer, Tag thought, Barlow was all right.

Back at the cavern, Tag met the captain in charge of the Ranger company and introduced Colonel Barlow to Giesla, Prentice, Sergeant Betcher, and the two graybeards in command of the partisans, while Bones, the medic, closed his wound with butterfly bandages, applied a fresh dressing, and prescribed APCs and extended bed rest.

"'Cause, Captain," the medic said, "that's the

only way I know to keep you from gettin' holes
punched in you, sir."

Tag let Giesla help him into a fresh jumpsuit
from one of the resupply boxes that dropped in
with the Rangers, then he said to Barlow, "Let's
go inside, Colonel. We've got maps and a situation
table in there."

Barlow, Giesla, Prentice, Betcher, and Wheels
followed him down the shaft to the cavern.

Barlow surveyed the makeshift sand table for
a moment in the light of the gas lanterns, then
spread an acetate-covered map from his own map
case on one corner and motioned the others in
closer.

"Two days ago," Barlow began, "elements of the
Warsaw Pact armies launched a tactical nuclear
strike against units of the French and American
armies here in SOUTHAG. Thanks largely to the
intelligence provided by this unit, the deception
that the Soviets had planned to lure our armies
into large concentrations, so they could be dev-
astated by the nuclear attack, failed. Neither, I
should add, did the Soviets have sufficient throw
weight to make their assault successful, even if
we had fallen for their ruse. Again, Captain, we
have you and your unit to thank for that. General
Kettle had enough confidence in all of you to
buck his entire staff—myself included, I'm sorry to say—and issued orders that pulled our field
armies back from their assault positions and out
of range of the worst of the nuclear detonations.
Our response, as you might well judge even from
this remove, was swift and total.

"The results of this exchange have been two-
fold, one military and the other political.

"Militarily, the situation would be relatively

simple, were it not for the nuclear element and
its political consequences." Barlow tapped on his
map as he continued: "The Soviets have lost
SOUTHAG, gentlemen . . . and ma'am. The only
remaining Soviet force of any consequence—core
elements of the First Guards Tank Army and two
former Czech divisions—is bottled up here in the
hilly plateau country north of Lake Constance.
The skeleton forces left here in the Jura to man
the nuclear launchers have been totally routed and
can offer no reinforcements. That also leaves us in
command of the Soviets' only line of retreat. The
French have reinforced our positions in the Black
Forest, and even the Russians would not violate
Swiss neutrality, at least not just for the privilege
of taking their tanks through the Alps."

"Sounds to me like fish in a barrel," Tag said.
"What's the problem, Colonel?"

"Primarily political," Barlow responded. "But
I'll come to that in a moment. First let me tell
you the good news. CENTAG has held. More than
that, the Soviets are being pushed back toward
Fulda, and we have already retaken Würzburg. In
the north, divisions from the Canadian, British,
German, and American armies have driven to the
River Weser and established forward positions
across it. As of midnight last night, they were
still fighting the clock to keep their bridges up
and move men into Lower Saxony. If they can hold
the bridgeheads and advance far enough to bring
Hannover under their guns, the Soviets' northern
army will be effectively cut off. At worst, we
will have extended Ivan's flank and made him
vulnerable to counterattacks."

"Colonel," Giesla said, "what do you mean
'fighting the clock'?"

"Ah," said Barlow, "that brings us to the political matters. In a nutshell, the politicians of both sides made allies of the generals on both sides when they ordered the nuclear option. Following our retaliatory strike, General Kettle contacted General Gloz, his counterpart in the Warsaw Pact, and offered him a moratorium on the use of nuclear weapons. Gloz, I must say, was only too happy to oblige. Realizing that their orders had appalled their own professional soldiers, the politicians stepped in. Not knowing the extent of our superiority on the battlefield following the exchange, our side agreed to a cease-fire, beginning tonight at twenty-four-hundred hours."

"The hell they did," Tag blurted.

"What are its terms?" Giesla asked calmly.

"Initially," Barlow answered, "it's to be limited to enough time for each side to evacuate its people from the radiation zones, but with fighting to halt all along the front."

"So who gets the better of that deal, sir?" Lieutenant Prentice asked.

"I'd say it's a push, Lieutenant," said Barlow. "It gives Ivan time to dig in and regroup, but it also gives us a window in which to bring over supplies from the states and equip the Brits' reserves. I don't mind telling you that, despite the successes I mentioned a moment ago, we were getting stretched damned thin. And with the Chinese sitting on their thumbs and grinning at Japan, the Russians might be willing to pull fresh divisions in from Mongolia and Siberia, even if it means losing parts of them. At this point, we just don't know for certain how desperate Ivan is. There's even some debate over who's in charge in the Kremlin right now."

"So," said Tag, "where does that leave us, sir?
Are we demobbed or decommissioned or deserted
or what?"

"Mmmm, well." Barlow cleared his throat.
"You're still under General Kettle's command,
Captain. But we'll speak of that privately." He
turned to the rest of the group. "If there are
no other questions, you will excuse the captain
and me."

As the briefing broke up, Tag led Colonel Barlow across the cavern to the plank tables where
the coffee urns sat next to platters of sausage and
bread and cheese.

"I see," said Barlow, "that you are suffering the
privations of war."

"Like Mao said," Tag replied, " 'you get by with
a little help from your friends.' "

Barlow cocked an eyebrow. "Mao said that, did
he? I've always wondered." He bit a large plug
from a cheese-and-sausage sandwich and chewed
it hungrily.

"So," Tag said, "what are these mysterious orders of mine, sir?"

Barlow mumbled something, took a drink of
coffee to clear his mouth, and said, "Pretty simple, actually, Max." Barlow took another sip of
coffee before going on. "We don't trust Ivan any
farther than you can shoot an oh-five with a
slingshot, right? And you'd better believe that
those troops bottled up down south don't give
a flying fornication about the cease-fire, not if
it means they're going to be stuck in the middle of that hellhole. I'm not even sure that they
could withdraw through the strike zones if we let
them. And that's the rub. You see, Gloz wants to
include the First Guards Tanks among those units

we have mutually agreed can be evacuated from the hot areas. But for a lot of reasons—not the least of which is their being the army that started this madness—Kettle will not go along with it. Ever. I think he would defy the President on this one, Max. But I'll deny it if you ever say I said so. You know the general, and you know how he feels about warfare. For a man as tough-minded and practical as he is, there's still a lot of Patton in him, the part that makes him both a visionary and a romantic. I think that the use of nuclear weapons represents to him some sort of breach of honor, the violation of some notion of war that may or may not be valid today. He's a great general, Max—I don't know of any other who could have done what he has done with so little—and I'm not judging him. But I think this has become something almost personal with him. That's why he wants his personal recon unit to carry out the orders I have for you."

"I'm still listening, sir," Tag said.

"What the general wants, Max, is two things. First, he wants firsthand ground-level intelligence on conditions in the dead zone—the effects of the nukes and the strength and disposition of the Soviet forces. Second—and this may turn out to be your first priority—he wants you in place to harass and interdict Ivan's attempts to probe the zone, to destroy any enemy targets you encounter, and prevent any movement that might jeopardize our positions while we are advancing and leaving thin spots in the line."

"And we're supposed to do all this with one tank, sir?"

"Yes and no, Max," Barlow said, taking another sip of coffee. "The XM-F4 is the only thing we have in this sector that can go close enough to the ground-zero points to be safe in there, especially now that the storm has scattered the fallout and the rain last night is still carrying thousands of RADs into hot spots of runoff. Your Jagd Kommandos can't get any closer to the zone than NBC suits will permit, but they can cover breakout points, maintain a temporary HQ, and may be able to supply backup. What you'll like better is the two Bradleys that will be here this afternoon."

Despite all his misgivings, Tag had been listening to Barlow with mounting anticipation. Already, a thousand possibilities for navigating and fighting on a nuclear battlefield were cascading through his mind. But none of them included Bradleys. Tag scratched his head.

"Okay, sir," he said. "We are down to one Bradley, and it's a bucket of bolts, but I don't see how they're going to be a lot of help in there, in the dead zone."

"Trust me, Captain," said Barlow. "These are not ordinary vehicles. The general knows what you need, and he had to do some very high-level arm twisting to see that you get it. There are mechanics and technicians from Fort Hood to Hereford to Brussels who all curse your name—or would, if they knew it. You will find ways to use these particular vehicles, I'm sure. Which reminds me: I hear you have a man with you who has distinguished himself quite admirably in a Bradley—a Sergeant Sain? I noticed that you didn't have him at the briefing, but I'd like to meet him."

"Colonel," Tag said, "let's sit down."

With no very great hope that he could adequate-

ly prepare Colonel Barlow for the (un)reality of
Sergeant M. N. Sain, Tag quickly recounted what
he knew of the mythomaniacal warrior, trying
hard to be objective and not sound apologetic. He
finished by ticking off N. Sain's battlefield accom-
plishments on his fingers, completely unnerved
by the grin that had been spreading across the
colonel's acorn-brown face.

"Wait, Max, wait," Barlow said, stopping Tag's
enumeration. "You mean his crew are in fact his
former drummer and keyboard player; he is a
reservist who happened to be here, playing in a
USO band so he could visit his old sidemen, when
the balloon went up; he speaks gibberish, and they
not at all; and he feeds hashish to prisoners during
interrogation? Is that about it?"

"No, sir," Tag said, resignation heavy in his
voice, "there's a lot more, but all that is true."

"Well, from what you say, he at least has taste
in music, Max." Barlow unfolded from the ammo
box where he was sitting. "Take me to him."

Mad Dog, N. Sain's Rastafarian-looking
drummer-cum-driver, was squatted in front of
his battle-scarred Bradley rapping out bomba-
diddles on a .50-caliber ammunition can, while
the two young blond twins from the veterinary
clinic looked on in shy delight.

"MD," Tag said, "where is the Disciple of Darkness?"

Mad Dog twirled the sticks, reached behind his
head without turning around, and hammered out
a riff on the nose of the vehicle. Then he whirled
them back and resumed his monotonous rolls on
the steel can.

Long-haired and unshaven, shirtless and glis-
tening with sweat, the hair on his chest and arms

plastered in windrows, N. Sain leaned out of the
forward hatch of the Bradley and eyed Barlow with
bemused indifference. To Tag he said, "He carries
himself like a Faustian, o Cousin of Kali, but he
has that look in his eye." He stared hard at Barlow.
"Are you," N. Sain demanded, "in deed or in fact
a slave of time or of your time or of times yet gone
or to come?"

Tag cringed, but Barlow answered evenly,
"Those are days of future past. But your rhythm
man plays Cream by rote."

N. Sain bounded from the hatch, sprang to
something like attention, grabbed Barlow's left
hand in both of his, and held it palm-first near his
face. "Ooo," he crooned, "ooo, look, look. The
hands of a master, calluses of the discipline. Is
rock and roll your life, o Believer?"

"The Army is my life," Barlow said reasonably,
"but music is my soul, and soul is my music."

"Captain Maximus," said N. Sain, sounding
both sane and serious, "this man is not one of
us; his soul is too pure. We are not worthy to
string his axe. Electric bass, right?"

Barlow nodded in self-satisfaction. "Barbero
Custom," he replied, "with four- and six-string
necks and a solid-state integrated amp."

"What the hell are you two talking about, sir?"
Tag asked.

"Oh, a hobby of mine," Barlow said. "Something I picked up in college. We even had a little
group together in Washington, when I was with
General Kettle there in '91. You may have heard
of us, The Dogs of War? Well, no time for that." He
faced back toward N. Sain. "Sergeant, I'm going to
see to it that you get a fresh number to really lay
down some heavy licks on Comrade Ivan."

N. Sain rolled his eyes. "O, to be all that I can be, to realize my essential oneness with annihilation and the cosmic rhythm. I am so grateful for the kindness of strangers." He snapped his heels together and executed a curt, Oriental bow.

"Later," Colonel Barlow replied with a languid wave of his hand and a surreptitious nod to Tag.

As they left N. Sain and his bomba-diddling drummer, Tag turned to Barlow and said, "Sir, I've been thinking, and I'm not sure I understand what's so hush-hush about my orders. It's about what we've been doing, isn't it?"

"Not what but where," Barlow said. "That's the difference. One of the stipulations of the cease-fire is that all dead zones be demilitarized, until after the evacuations, at least. As far as SACEUR is concerned, you are off your maps and outside orders."

"Which means no logistical support, right, sir?"

"No. We'll maintain air- and ground-supply options, but we can't supply air cover or any regular troops to help you out, and we can't extract you."

Tag shrugged. "So, what's new?" he said. "One more thing, Colonel: our foot troops. Prentice's kids have taken about fifty percent casualties since we first picked them up, and we could use some fresh horses there."

"Take a platoon of Rangers," Barlow suggested.

"I'd rather stick with Prentice and whatever he can muster, maybe get a top kick and another NCO, plus some replacements, from the Rangers, if that's okay."

"Done," the angular colonel said. "Meanwhile, Max, get your tank and your crew rounded up. We have a couple of technicians with us who need to put a few new bells and whistles on your XM-F4."

Spotting Ham and Fruits in the mess area, Tag veered from Barlow's side, saying, "I'll meet you outside."

The cargo containers held all sorts of trimmings for the No Slack Too. There were special filters for the ventilation systems, aerosol canisters of decontaminant spray, additional supplies of NBC suits and gas masks, cans of a sooty paint designed to absorb radiation and hold it when washed off, synthetic-rubber boots for the gun mantles on the main tube and the Phalanx, resupplies of ammunition and lubricants, fresh racks of War Club missiles, and a box of computer disks with upgraded programs for all the systems on the No Slack Too.

Fruits rifled through a box of diskettes, whistled breathily, and said, "Now lookitis shit. We gotchur basic twenty-four-hour satellite television. We gotchur full-freak radio bands. We gotchur integrated-systems tahget image. We gotchur IR suppressers, your multi-tahget coordinator, and somekinda avionics bullshit."

Tag said to Barlow, "Are we supposed to be flight-capable, too, now, sir?"

The young technician who sat in the No Slack Too's commander's chair, loading the programs into the XM-F4's twin computer systems, looked up and grinned at the tank crew assembled outside.

"Not quite, sir," he said to Tag. "This is a program modified from the Doppler navigation software we use in helicopters, all right, but in your case it's tied to the LandNav system. If you have just a single known point of reference, it'll give you an exact fix on yourself in, oh, about ten nanoseconds."

"Hey, Tutti," Ham Jefferson said, "how long is ten nanoseconds, whiz kid?"

Fruits screwed his head to one side like a bird in thought, then said, "Ah, about eighteen or nineteen feet."

Barlow turned to Tag and asked, "Did I miss something?"

"An old joke," Tag said, "from the naive days when Tutti used to try to teach these other barbarians something about electronics and physics. Eighteen feet, that's about how far light travels in ten nanoseconds."

"Hilarious," Barlow deadpanned.

"Yeah," Tag said, "I guess you had to be there."

One of the Rangers came loping over to the No Slack Too and told Barlow that the Bradleys were arriving.

"Send them on down here," the colonel told the runner, then said to Tag, "Come on, Captain. There's nothing for you to do here until all that software's installed. I'll give you a sneak peek at the Bradleys you'll be working with."

Tag had to scramble to keep pace with the colonel's long stride across the jumbled tailings. He was so busy watching his step that he heard the Bradleys before he saw them. Looking up, he paused in his tracks, goggling as he tried to take in what he saw. Barlow glanced back and pursed his lips in amusement at Tag's reaction.

They were Bradleys, all right, the extended versions called muscle models; that much was clear from their profiles. But nothing else quite matched up in Tag's mind. Their sound was a turbine moan, not the clatter of diesel. The nose and sides on the Bradleys were sheathed in a dull-glinting armor that Tag felt sure could only be slick skin. The multiple barrels of a 20mm chain gun protruded from a coaxial mount on the nose, and on top, where the 75mm turret should have been, there was the low dome of a Phalanx cupola, identical to the one on the turret of the No Slack Too. On either side of the cupola, mounted flush with the top deck, were pods of stubby antitank missiles.

"Well, come on, Captain," Barlow said. "I thought tankers didn't like to walk. Let's hitch a ride, and I'll show you around."

Tag quickly found that these Bradleys were as far removed from other armored personnel-carriers as the No Slack Too was from other tanks. He had seen something like them on the drawing boards at Hood, but didn't know that the infantry was this far advanced, even in prototypes.

"In fact, Max," Barlow told him, "these are what you might call protoprototypes. The turbine-powered chassis were swiped from your leg com-rades; the monopolar armor came straight from the foundry; we bootlegged all the electronics and armaments from your old project at Hood; and the whole thing was assembled at Hereford."

"How much shakedown time on them?" Tag asked as he fiddled with the Bradley's fire-control console.

"Oh, about thirty nanoseconds."

"Pardon."

"We drove them on and off the aircraft, Max. That's it. But the chassis and turbines have been checked out."

Tag sighed and shrugged, as if to say, "Why did I ask?"

"But speaking of that," Barlow went on, "Colonel Menefee asked me to be sure to get a copy of your evaluation log for the XM-F4."

"Sir," Tag said, "please tell Colonel Menefee that I'll fax it to him."

"I'll do that, Captain," said Barlow, "next time I think about it. I certainly will."

Tag returned his grin.

The technician had finished loading the No Slack Too's computers when Tag, Barlow, and the two Bradleys rumbled up beside it. Fruits was in the commander's chair, showing off the systems on the VLD for Lieutenant Prentice, who was leaning through the open hatch. The Ranger captain was also nearby, directing the dispositions of the prisoners taken in the skirmish, and the three Jagd Kommando gun buggies were making their way back from the wood line.

"Max," Barlow said, "it looks like we have most of the players together, so let's rally them up. I'll go over the hardware with everyone, and we can sort out some replacements for your strike platoon."

"Sounds good to me, sir," Tag said.

Tag and Barlow dismounted, collected Prentice, and called over the Ranger captain, whom Barlow introduced as Butch Lawrence, a towheaded Alabamian who would be in charge of permanent security for the raiders' base at the mine works. The colonel explained what they needed, and the Ranger said to Prentice, "Come on, Lieutenant. We'll do a little shopping."

Giesla wheeled her echelon of three vehicles into place adjacent to the XM-F4 and the Bradleys and joined Tag and Barlow. She was still driving one car herself, with the lightly wounded Horst in the loader's seat. Betcher and Karl manned the second vehicle, and Jan and Uwe the third. They still had two full racks of ATGMs inside the cavern, and Tag was again amazed at how durable the lightly armored gun buggies had proved to be.

Barlow tapped a salute on the edge of his helmet. "Nice piece of work," he said to Giesla.

"Thank you, sir," she said. "We have been having a lot of practice."

"Well," Tag said, "I hope they're ready for some more, Gies."

"What is that?" she asked.

"I'll explain it all when Chuck gets back; you'll both need to hear. Right now, Colonel Barlow wants to show you some hardware he's brought along."

While the technicians and the crew of the No Slack Too were coating the tank and the Bradleys with the radioactive-absorbent paint and replacing hatch seals and ventilation filters, Colonel Barlow directed the reequipping of the Jagd Kommandos. There were no towed missile racks among the boxes that came in with the Rangers, but there were ATGM arrays that attached to the roll cages of the gun buggies and .223 mini-guns fitted on detachable mounts that bolted to the nose armor. Along with resupplies of ammunition for the 106mm recoilless rifles and the naval-mounted .50-caliber, there were fiberglass cowls with bat-wing doors to enclose the cockpits, the absorbent paint for the exteriors, and new self-sealing honeycomb tires. The technicians tuned all three of the fuel-injected Porsche motors and also contrived to rebuild the damaged front suspension on Giesla's vehicle.

As the work on the gun buggies was going on,

Prentice returned with Captain Lawrence and a squad of Rangers from his company, sixteen men, a squad leader, and a master sergeant to replace Weintaub, Prentice's topkick, who had been killed in action. Prentice introduced the master sergeant as Krager and the E-5 squad leader as Villalobos.

"I remember you, Captain," Villalobos said to Tag. "You were at the Ranger School when I went through in '91."

"Glad to have you with us," Tag said, shaking the sergeant's hand. "You came out of a good crop." He looked to Master Sergeant Krager and said, "And you've done the impossible, Gaylord; I think you're actually uglier than the last time I saw you."

"And to you, too, Ma . . . *Captain* Max." Krager leaned forward and shook Tag's free hand.

"I see you all know one another," Captain Lawrence said.

"Yeah," Tag said. "And thanks, Butch. I'll go to war with these guys any time."

Prentice assembled his Rangers—the replacements and his veterans—and moved them inside the cavern to finish rationing the gear and to reorganize the unit, as N. Sain, Mad Dog, and Rabies, all barefoot and shirtless, came blinking out of the cavern and into the sunlight, oblivious to the goggling Ranger replacements.

"Don't ask," Tag said to Lawrence. Then he shouted to Fruits, "Hey, Tutti, show our friends the mystic magic of the new machines, will you?"

"Awright, awright," Fruits responded, waving his hand out the hatch of the No Slack Too. "I'll do dat, *too*."

The men ate in shifts throughout the afternoon and finished the modifications to the vehicles by

1600 hours, when Barlow called the final briefing.
He let Tag outline as much as necessary about the
details of the mission, then wished them all luck
and suggested they turn in early. At 0300, they
would be heading out, and he did not have to
remind them where.

3

Colonel Feyodr Oblanovich Yeshev was not a happy man, and in that, at least, he was like every other soldier of the First Guards Tank Army. Unlike them, he knew what had gone wrong and why. He knew before the first nuclear device exploded that of the three possible outcomes—victory, stalemate, and defeat—two were bad. Yeshev was enough of a gambling man to trust the odds, and they had run to form, leaving the military situation balanced on the head of a pin, the slightest shift enough to topple the field to either side, although possessing that field might not be worth the game. A commando by temperament and a tank killer by training, Yeshev had never been comfortable with the Grand Gambit, the high command's inflexible strategy involved in shifting whole armies to try to gain a battlefield advantage for a nuclear strike alone, one that had two chances in three of failing in its intent. Indeed, like most field commanders, he shuddered at the thought of nuclear weapons on the battlefield, and all his worst fears had been exceeded by the reality of atomic warfare.

He knew that their fate was sealed when Moscow elected to go forward with the nuclear option even after those American tank comman-

dos—whoever they were—had destroyed almost
three-fourths of the warheads intended for the
principal launch positions. But no one, not even
Yeshev, foresaw the massive throw weight or the
lethal accuracy with which the NATO allies were
able to respond. The crags and narrow valleys
where the First Guards took up positions, in the
mountains and rugged plateau land between the
Danube and Lake Constance, had offered good
protection from the initial blasts of counterfire,
and the driving storm that followed had carried
some of the worst of the fallout past the Soviets.
But the effects on their advance units—and, ulti-
mately, on the army's strategic options—had been
devastating, nearly total. His sole consolation was
in knowing that the NATO Allies could no more
penetrate the atomic swath than the Soviets were
capable of breaking through it in any sort of defen-
sible formation.

From the few blistered satellite images and the
various firsthand reports that Yeshev had gathered, he had a reasonably accurate idea of what had
happened in the nuclear exchange. The Allies had
not taken the bait of the false front with its disguised array of launchers. Instead of massing for
an attack, they had dispersed and withdrawn out
of range. Cruise missiles swarming out of Germany and France had concentrated on the reinforced
positions farther south, here in the mountains and
the ravines of the plateau. The forward elements
of the Tank Guards had been annihilated, almost
seventy percent of their armor destroyed. His own
regiment, the core of the army's antitank and
reconnaissance forces, which had been held in
reserve, was largely intact but scattered and iso-
lated by the hot spots of radiation, which were still

playing hell with radio traffic. And if that were not enough, those huge damned American satellites that had for almost two years been passively gathering data on the solar wind also turned out to be weapons platforms whose massive collection panels had provided power to the concealed lasers that had blasted seven of the Soviet Union's twelve observation and communications satellites out of space.

Shit! Yeshev thought, slamming his fist down on the fender of his T-80B, one of the handful of the top-secret tanks that he had under his command. In the fury of his thoughts, he had been breathing like a locomotive, and the moisture from his breath was condensing inside the bulky NBC suit he wore, turning his neck clammy where it touched the accordion folds of the fabric. Not only was his unit scattered and unable to communicate effectively but he had now to consider the implications of those unanticipated tank commandos who had been largely the cause of the current situation—at least as much as those Tartar-brained idiots of the high command. Under almost any other conditions, Yeshev would have relished the presence of a worthy opponent, an enemy who would try the expertise, valor, and technology of his regiment. But in the reports he received from the survivors of the escort columns that the Allied commandos had foiled, he recognized not only the presence of a tank that was perhaps the equal of his own T-80B but also the tactical principles of that damned Ross Kettle, the barbarian half-breed who—damn his eyes—was the guru of tank warfare. On the battlefield that Yeshev saw in his mind's eye, there was no clear advantage for him, no matter how many pieces of armor he possessed. Any tanker as skilled and brave as the one he believed he faced would be a problem, but with a tank the equivalent of his own operating according to Kettle's book, there were no precedents, no simulations to prepare his men for it. That damned American tank and its support vehicles had left him in a position to take the blame for the blunders of the Kremlin, and his only choice now was to take direct command of the current mission to see that it did not happen again. General Tsarchev would, Yeshev felt sure, have no qualms about a summary execution if he failed.

Yeshev was one of the few Soviet commanders who had read, understood, and admired Kettle's books. Usually dismissed as a dreamer of powerful imagination, Kettle was generally underestimated by the Soviet general staff, who called his "speculative armor" science fiction and thought the principles of combat built around that armor purely wishful thinking, far beyond the actual capabilities of Western technology. And, even granting the possibility of quantum leaps in tank design, they continued to disregard the tactics, calling down upon them that most damning of Communist curses, bourgeois liberalism, for much of the success of Kettle's ideas depended upon the individual initiative and adaptability to circumstances of each tank commander and crew. Even Yeshev, schooled as he was in traditional Soviet military science, had to concede some reservations—for Soviet crews. But he had once spent two weeks at Fort Hood when he was a young captain, in the salad days of *glasnost*, and he knew enough of American soldiers not to be surprised by any audacity.

But, he wondered, did that audacity and that technology extend to probing the dead zone of radiation? He did not know, and that worried him. He stared distractedly at the tank and BMP crews who, all dressed in the bulky NBC suits, were servicing the machines of his headquarters company, which lay stretched along the steep ravine he had chosen for them in which to wait out the nuclear aftermath. Was he now the hunted instead of the hunter?

As Yeshev stood there, rapt in these thoughts and now breathing normally, his wool gathering was interrupted by the appearance of his intelligence officer, a major named Viktor, from the Ukrainian Republic, whom Yeshev had long suspected of being a mole and toady for the KGB political officer. The major's sly, knowing expression was only half-hidden behind the visor of his suit and was patent in his voice as he handed Yeshev the onionskin burn sheets containing the latest intelligence estimates, the last he would receive before launching his mission.

"Comrade Colonel," the major said, "I think this should be all you need to complete your part in the glorious victory that waits at hand."

"Don't speak to me of glory, Nikolai," Yeshev said good-humoredly. "We both know where that path leads. At this point, I would think that you, of all people, should be pleased to know that we can even survive. Have you seen the latest satellite images?"

Major Viktor shrugged. "Worthless," he said. "Everything we have here is from human assets. The situation is much better than we originally projected, Comrade Colonel, far too good to warrant any defeatist pessimism."

Yeshev rolled the papers into a baton and slapped them lightly in his hand. "Yes?" he said. "Tell me, then, what is the cause of this optimism? Has the general staff arranged a cossack charge, perhaps, or discovered a cache of flying carpets in Turkistan?"

The major's face fell into a censorious scowl. "I would not," he said, "speak lightly of those who have led us in this glori—in this victorious campaign against the capitalist aggressors, Comrade Colonel. They have many ears."

"Yes," Yeshev agreed blandly. "Twice as many as they have ass holes. Go on Nikolai."

"Our strike has immobilized the NATO ground forces," Viktor continued. "They are withdrawing on all fronts. Their commander, your darling aborigine, was first to sue for the cease-fire. But now he is foolishly attempting to block the political negotiations for our retre—redeployment. Even with the air drop, Kettle has less than a division between us and the Czech border. Even better, we have it on very good authority that there is only one unit of tank commandos probing the strike zone—just enough for your amusement, I would think, Comrade Colonel."

If you could think, Yeshev said to himself. Then, aloud, he said, "And does your 'very good authority' also know what that one unit did to our convoy, how it and it alone brought the Grand Gambit to this stalemate? Nikolai, Nikolai"— Yeshev shook his head—"your politics are quite correct and your patriotism unquestioned, but you must never be contemptuous of a proven enemy. Indifferent, perhaps, but never contemptuous, not as long as that enemy is still in the field. Is there any word yet from our lost patrol?"

"The survivors of the imperialist ambush?" Viktor shook his head. "We have received some phantom transmissions that could have been theirs, but nothing definite. Why, Comrade Colonel?"

"They are our only firsthand assets, if we can bring them in, who can tell us anything about this American unit," Yeshev said. "And it's very important that we know, Nikolai—very important that *I* know. What about our maps?"

"In the operations bunker, Comrade Colonel. I asked them to make you overlays from the situation table. They will be ready by noon."

Yeshev's face set in an amused scowl, one he knew Viktor could discern through the visor. He had failed to ask the major for overlays, and now Viktor would make him wait for them. It was the kind of smug, self-serving, mean-spirited thing the Ukrainian did that made Yeshev want to rip Nikolai Viktor's lungs out.

"Thank you," he said. "I will also want to see all of the most recent satellite and atmospheric-reconnaissance photographs, no matter how worthless, Nikolai. Tell operations that I will need those overlays before noon. You can do that when you deliver the reconnaissance photos, *da*?"

The major stiffened, straightening the wrinkles in his NBC suit. "Of course, Comrade Colonel," he replied. "Anything else?"

"Not for now, Nikolai, thank you."

Yeshev eyed Major Viktor's back narrowly as the intelligence officer walked awkwardly across the muddy, sloping face of the ravine. Viktor was a perfect example of the New Soviet, which was in fact old Marxist wine in new authoritarian bottles.

Just as in the old days, Viktor had risen in the army through the Party, political orthodoxy taking the place of professional expertise, although Yeshev had to admit that he was not incompetent, only hidebound and more fearful of the Party apparatus than of the NATO armies. And perhaps he had good reason, for the internal security forces, primarily the KGB, had gained an ascendancy within the new Soviet Union that would have been the envy of every KGB chief up to and including Andropov, whose name, associated as it was with that of Gorbachev, had become anathema to the political watchdogs of the KGB. All that Gorbachev's purges of the so-called hard-liners within the security forces had accomplished was to push the real threat deeper within the system, like latent diseases just waiting their opportunity to strike and spread.

But Yeshev was, unquestionably, a patriot, a true son of Mother Russia. Born in Tula, south of Moscow, Yeshev could trace his family's military tradition back nearly two hundred years, to the Napoleonic Wars, when no fewer than five Yeshevs had fought in the Czar's army against Bonaparte. His great-great grandfather had been a gunner at Sevastopol, his grandfather a brigade commander with the original Red Army, and his father, still a teenager, emerged from the siege of Leningrad as a brevet captain and later was rewarded with a regular commission and a military scholarship. Yeshev had never for one moment imagined that he would be anything but a soldier. Too young for Afghanistan, he received his commission on the very eve of the great "restructuring" that fragmented the Soviet Union, politically and economically.

Yeshev pretended to read the optimistic assessments printed on the burn sheets in his hand, but his mind could not disengage itself from contemplation of everything that had brought him and his country to this. It had taken nearly a decade for the reforms of Gorbachev and Svetlov to fall finally into irrevocable disrepute, and he, like many Russians and others in the Union, held the West much to account for that fall from progressive grace. True, old habits of shoddy work and bureaucratic mismanagement had lingered on within the Soviet infrastructure. Production never quite kept pace with demand or wages with prices. Western technological assistance was always one generation behind the leading edge, especially in electronics from Japan, whose leaders had no qualms about holding it hostage to a set of humiliating demands for the return of the Kuril Islands, which lie between the Kamchatka Peninsula and the Japanese home island of Hokkaido. Worse, in the minds of most Russians, however, had been the economic vindictiveness of Western Europe and the United States.

Despite slow growth and a host of internal stresses—religious, political, and nationalistic—Russia had more than kept pace with the creeping prosperity of its erstwhile satellites. Reforms in management and distribution had largely put an end to shortages of critical consumer goods, such as meat, bread, oil, and toilet paper, but *glasnost* in the press had also opened the people's eyes to how far behind they still lagged. Greater freedom of travel had also meant that more and more citizens could see the disparity firsthand, just a train ride away in West Germany. Still, Russia was producing and was

exporting. Fiat and Ford had both established
factories in Russia to produce cars for the entire European market, and Russia itself had done
an excellent job of promoting its famed luxury items—furs, caviar, premium vodkas, and
more recently, watches and jewelry. They had
likewise made inroads in international construction, and it was this that precipitated the cri-
sis.

Especially in the Middle East, even in many
of those countries with strong ties to the old
USSR, the British, French, and Americans had
dominated the nonindigenous major construction
projects, often with the use of cheap Asian labor
from Korea and Taiwan. Under *perestroika*, the
elimination of tens of thousands of redundant or
superfluous jobs had created a huge labor surplus
of unskilled or semiskilled workers that were
a serious drain on the government's budget for
domestic improvements. It was Svetlov's genius
to realize that, even operating at a marginal loss,
state construction companies could absorb many
of the displaced workers in foreign projects. As
zero-sum enterprises, they could compete suc-
cessfully for the contracts and at the same time
relieve the government of most of the expense
of providing relief for the workers, while at the
same time establishing Russia as a major player in the construction market. Unfortunately, it
worked too well.

The isolationist Congress of the United States,
under pressure from American builders, took the
position that this success was a sign that the
United States had been too generous with its
aid and concessions to Russia. Aid was reduced,
loans called in, and measures were passed to allow

American businesses to play the kind of entrepreneurial hardball that they know best. Soon Russia was losing bids and had to drastically scale back its foreign projects, casting thousands out of work and onto the mean streets of Moscow in the bitter winter of 1995–96.

It really began in the late spring and summer of 1995, while Yeshev had been on leave and staying with friends who managed a large communal farm just west of Tula. The previous winter had been unnaturally warm and dry, and the wheat had not properly stooled, leaving the prospects for the year's crop at best mediocre. One morning, Yeshev went riding with his friends, on the pretext of inspecting the crop, but in fact for the sheer pleasure of being on horseback upon the plains of Russia. It was a cool, dry morning, with only the arcs of mare's-tail clouds to break up the blue of the sky. But before noon, those clouds had begun to crowd together like fish gills, and by lunch the sky was bruised with dark, angry-looking thunderheads. Yeshev and his friends were within sight of the barn when the first hailstones fell.

Even without the promise of oats in the barn, the horses would not have had to be spurred, for balls of ice larger than crab apples were whistling out of the sky like grapeshot before the riders made the safety of the commune offices. The storm rose in a deafening cacophony, maddening horses in their stalls, killing livestock in the fields, and drowning out all but shouted conversation, as hail continued to pour from the sky, some of it as large as a man's head. The car Yeshev had come in had its window glass shattered and its body pocked as though a hundred mad hammerers had turned on it. There was

nothing to do but stand away from the windows
and watch in silence as the ice accumulated,
sometimes to a depth of more than two feet,
and beat down the sparse green wheat that was
just beginning to make heads. Throughout the
eastern plain, the story was much the same. And
in the Siberian plain, west of the Urals, the story was equally bad: drought and flood claimed
more than fifty percent of the grain crops. More
than a million head of livestock, including dairy
herds, had to be destroyed for lack of food. It
was the most widespread natural disaster of the
century.

That winter, there were bread riots in every
major city in Russia. The weather was brutal,
and entire villages were faced with starvation for
the first time since Stalin. Svetlov might have
survived the economic pressures, Yeshev thought,
but, as English Prime Minister Disraeli once said,
any politician who cannot control the weather
cannot be expected to control the people. When
Svetlov agreed to step aside, in a move that surprised most Russians not aware of the infighting
and power struggles within the Party, there were
radically reactionary elements already poised to
leap into the breach.

Yeshev had read enough history to see the par-
allels between what came next and the worst
years of the French Revolution, especially those
last months of 1793, known as The Terror. But
unlike the hydra-headed upheaval in France, the
second Communist "revolution" in Russia had
a guiding genius, a cabal of hardliners deeply
entrenched in key ministries, most notably the
KGB, which operated more or less openly in the
guise of the Lenin Political Clubs. Ostensibly,

these clubs were no more than forums for political debate and discussion, and many of their members were genuine intellectuals whose involvement in politics was limited to the club, the café, and the classroom. In fact, every one of these clubs represented a cadre, a cell of unregenerate Marxist–Leninists who longed for the authoritarian iron fist of the "old" regime. When nature and the West conspired to make the time right for the "old thinkers," they recognized it and took to the streets. Mobilizing the clubs—and through them many students, intellectuals, and minor Party members, as well as the usual collection of thugs and bullyboys—the devotees of repression used the tactics of public protest, then available in the last days of *glasnost,* to fill Red Square with a howling mob of deprived Muscovites, displaced peasants, and agents provocateurs, forcing Svetlov into hasty retirement.

News of all this reached Yeshev slowly. He was then in command of a tank battalion at the edge of the Gobi Desert in Outer Mongolia and did not realize from the sketchy information in the official military dispatches the magnitude of what was going on in the capital, and the BBC world-service frequency that he had been monitoring to improve his English was suddenly jammed. Yeshev had been carefully apolitical in the army, and he knew when he was finally recalled to European Russia in the spring, when the coup was essentially over, that it was in part to test the "correctness" of his political posture. A practical professional, he had the sense to make reassuring mouth noises for the Party bosses and KGB hatchet men who grilled him about his readiness to fight for the renewal of Communist rule and Russian hegemony in its "historic sphere of influence," as Eastern Europe was euphemistically called in the Kremlin then.

As an officer of the Freedom Forces that, bit by bit, occupied and reintegrated the countries of the all but moribund Warsaw Pact, Yeshev knew he was being watched and assessed. He had done everything asked of him, however, and only the political tepidness of his early career and his barely disguised professional disdain for armchair theoreticians had kept him from becoming a staff officer. Which was just what Yeshev wanted. He cared about Russia, not about politics. He made war, not policy.

And, he decided as he rolled the onionskin intelligence report back into a tube, he had best be about it.

Yeshev's regimental operations center was a lead-lined, sandbagged bunker cut deep into one wall of the ravine. The ceiling was low and the air wetly ripe with the sweat of unwashed soldiers. Still, it came as a relief to Yeshev when he peeled off the cowl of his NBC suit and stood blinking for a moment in the hard white light of the fluorescent tubes that illuminated the situation room. Viktor had second-guessed him and was already there, aping a semblance of hectic energy as he huddled with the operations officer over a fan of grainy satellite and aerial photographs spread out on a bench to one side of the contoured situation table. Junior officers and NCOs were busily relaying messages from the bank of radios and computer terminals along one wall to other junior officers and NCOs, who glanced up nervously from their work on the sand table when Yeshev appeared. He waved them back to their jobs and crossed the bunker to where Viktor and Major Minski, the operations officer, were standing.

Minski, a tall, bespectacled man with the distracted air of an academician, made no pretense of wanting to be anywhere but back in his old lecture hall at the war college. He had an encyclopedic grasp of military history, strategy, and tactics and absolutely no imagination. An odd quality for an operations officer, but he was cautiously thorough and made up for his lack of creativity with an astounding catalog of obscure battles and stratagems that he could call upon when orchestrating the regimental plans. Yeshev liked him. Minski and Viktor straightened and turned to face their commander.

Nodding to Viktor, in recognition of his tacit surrender in this battle of their war of wills, Yeshev said to Minski, "I hope you have some wisdom of the ages for me, Professor."

"And I hope," Minski replied, "that you will settle for the guesses of the moment, Comrade Colonel." He essayed a wan smile. "Without knowing the size and dispositions of the enemy, operations are exceedingly difficult to plan, and without that same knowledge of one's own forces, almost impossible. But we are not the first army in history to encounter this situation, if my memory serves me."

"And I am certain that it does," Yeshev said quickly, to head off the explication of some remote battle that he knew would follow unless he did. "But what do we do to make our own history, here and now?"

"Ah," Minski said, arching his brows, "first we seek knowledge. Here, look first at these."

He scooped up the photos off the bench beside

him and handed them to Yeshev.

"These," the operations officer continued, "are the best we have from our eyes in the sky, but they are not so rheumy as they look, if you will examine the details I have circled."

Yeshev studied the images in question intently. Even without a magnifier he could make out the silhouettes of vehicles, both wheeled and tracked, as well as villages, fields, and forests, but he had no idea where they were from or whose army he was seeing.

"These," said Minski, anticipating Yeshev's questions, "were taken by one of our high-altitude aircraft just this morning—I've only received them from Major Viktor a few minutes ago—but you can clearly see that those are from one of our units."

Yeshev grunted. "Where?" he asked.

"About eighty kilometers northwest of here."

"And these others?" Yeshev asked, shuffling the photos and pulling out another.

"Those, I believe, are your American tank commandos."

Yeshev's head snapped up, like that of a hound catching a scent. "And do you know where?"

"Step to the table, please, Comrade Colonel," Viktor interjected.

The men working around the situation table stepped away, and Minski, assuming his professorial prerogative, brushed Viktor aside with his clear, authoritative voice.

"Here," he said, pointing with one of the long spatulas used to shape the wet sand on the table, "is where we sighted the main body of what we believe is the lost patrol, just entering this village called Grabbe. Some other images, from the satellites, also indicate that part of the patrol may still be here"—he swept over a forested area on the south bank of the Danube—"but this is at least a half guess. If they are in there, however, they may yet make contact with the Americans. The photo you have there, Comrade Colonel, was taken just as the Americans were entering these woods this morning about dawn."

"But they are to the east of the nuclear zone, *da*?"

"Correct, Comrade Colonel. There is little we can do for them one way or the other."

"What about these others, here at—what?— Grabbe?" Yeshev asked. "How do we get to them?"

"Come," Minski said. "The overlays should tell you that."

A large map of southern Germany that had been glued to a sheet of particleboard hung on one wall of the bunker. Yeshev and Viktor stood before it while Minski carefully taped an acetate sheet over it. The overlay was a motley of reds, yellows, and greens, indicating the relative levels of radiation. It was mostly red and yellow. One of the larger green zones contained the village of Grabbe.

"As you can see," said Minski, stepping away from the map, "once you move north of here, it is possible to travel between the two zones of contamination"—he pointed to the parallel lines that marked the Soviet and Allied strikes—"and work your way into Grabbe from the west. This will not be easy, Comrade Colonel, because the country is quite rough and heavily wooded in places, but that is where you have a clean corridor into Grabbe."

"But in the photographs," Yeshev said, "we see

our patrol entering from the other side. So there must be a way through the strike zone from the east or northeast as well."

Minski shrigged. "That is an assumption, but we have no knowledge of it," he said. "Many of the yellow areas on the overlay are at best hopeful guesses."

"But if they did enter from that direction, then the Americans could as well," Yeshev said. It was not a question, and neither Viktor nor Minski answered.

"Professor," Yeshev said, facing Minski, "I want those overlays in my map case in one hour. We are going to be leaving as soon as possible. And Nikolai," he said to Victor, "go over those aerial and satellite pictures again. They may not be so worthless as we thought, *da*?"

Yeshev resealed his NBC suit and left the operations bunker, already apprehensive about the mission and hoping they could snatch the patrol from Grabbe without encountering the Americans. He desperately needed to debrief the patrol and gather as much firsthand intelligence from them as he could. Otherwise he would be blundering about like a blind man in a mine field, one even more treacherous than the political booby traps with which the general staff had surrounded him. He felt that the entire blame for the disaster of the Grand Gambit was being subtly shifted to his shoulders. If he failed to find a way to extricate the First Guards—or what remained of it—from their nuclear cul-de-sac, his almost certain execution would leave him a handy scapegoat, unless they wanted a show trial first.

Yeshev had assembled his two-dozen best crews for the operation, twelve in the small 2S9-type tanks, and twelve in T-80s, plus his own T-80B, which, with its sophisticated electronics and communications systems, would act as their command center. Fuel might prove a problem for the larger armor, but Yeshev had decided even before the intelligence briefing that he would not take any fuel tanks in tow. The T-80s had sufficient range for what he now had in mind, and he found speed more desirable than distance in this case.

He passed along his orders for the new departure time, wrote a letter to his wife to leave with Minski, assembled his personal gear, and led his squadron out of the ravine at 0945.

4

That morning, just before daylight, as Tag made the decision to cut through the woods on the south bank of the Danube, instead of skirting their edge, one of the five surviving Soviet spy satellites passed overhead and in one frame caught the image of Tag's vehicles disappearing into the trees, the same photo that Yeshev held in his hands two hours later.

With the Jagd Kommandos at point and the Bradleys on the flanks, the raiders were making good time, now that the sun was up. Tag stood in the turret of the No Slack Too, breathing the cool, dry air that had followed the front in from the north. It was already autumn here in these highlands, where some of the hardwood trees had begun to lose their leaves, and he had to force himself to believe that they were less than thirty kilometers from a swath of nuclear destruction larger than anything like it that the world had known since the Huns scorched the earth from Asia to the Balkans.

His reverie was broken by the pop of the TacNet frequency in his CVC.

"Butcher Boy, this is Meat Grinder," he heard Giesla's voice say. "Over."

"This is Butcher Boy Actual," Tag replied. "Go."

"Butcher Boy, we have recent tracks of an estimated four—I say again, four—pieces of light armor that appear to be moving in front of us and in our same direction. Over."

"Roger, Meat Grinder. Put one of your units in advance and keep me posted. Butcher Boy out."

Tag put his raiders on alert and had them increase their flank intervals by fifty meters, shortening the echelon and spreading its front. The light was full now, and this patch of forest had been maintained as a woodlot, leaving a lot of big timber with open alleys through it, so it was easy for Tag to maintain visual contact with the Bradleys and catch an occasional glimpse of the Jagd Kommando gun vehicles in the van. As he directed the Bradleys into position, Tag could not help wondering what sort of détente Gaylord Krager had worked out with N. Sain in the super-Bradley on his right.

Krager had been in and out of the Army at least three times that Tag knew of, beginning with a hitch in Vietnam, when he had to lie about his age to be old enough to join, and most recently just before Operation Golden Spike in Central America, when he had to lie about his age to be young enough to serve. A real old-time soldier, Krager was stout, ugly, disciplined, brawling, professional, and insubordinate to junior officers. Between enlistments, he had brokered gun deals in the Middle East, trained rangers for the Royal Thai Army (he wore a winged elephant done in seed pearls on his dress uniform—the gaudy, official Royal Thai jump wings), worked security for a dozen international corporations, and built chicken houses in Kansas. Tag had met Krager four years ago at the Ranger School, where they were both training trainers, and what he still recalled most about the man was his incredible charm. Plug-ugly and coarse as a cob around the barracks, Krager could brief senior officers with the aplomb and diction of a diplomat or have twenty-five-year-old secretaries wilting all over his hairy arms. He danced like a dream and was the best knife fighter Tag ever knew, Ham Jefferson not excepted. Tag gave a mental shrug. Surely, he thought, somewhere in that bag of talents, Gaylord had the stuff to deal with Sain.

Tag looked to his left to check Prentice's position at the same moment that the TacNet popped through his CVC, followed by the voice of the Jagd Kommando Jan in the advance scout car.

"Butcher Boy, this is Meat Grinder Three. We have audio contact with tracked vehicles, six-zero-zero meters at your eleven o'clock."

"Roger, Grinder Three. Stay close, but don't scare them off."

"Roger, Butcher Boy. Meat Grinder Three out."

Tag immediately ordered the Bradleys out another fifty meters to allow the other two gun vehicles to drop back into the slots, while the No Slack Too moved forward to fill the middle. With the turbine-powered Bradleys and the repairs and refittings on the gun buggies, they were a surprisingly quiet unit, and Tag increased their speed. He could feel his chest just beginning to tighten with adrenaline, that warm, familiar tingling along the backs of his ears. He dropped through the turret hatch, dogged it behind him, swung down through the turret and into his seat. He opened the commander's hatch and elevated his chair to see over the glacis.

"All systems up," Tag said to his crew. "Arm all weapons. HE in the main tube, Mister Tutti."

"A done deal," Fruits said as the loading carousel spun and the breech fell into place.

Tag and Wheels cocked their coaxial machine guns, and the Phalanx barrels snapped once in rotation.

"All weapons systems are fine and primed, Boss," Ham Jefferson said.

The TacNet cut in, and Jan reported visual contact with the unidentified vehicles at five hundred meters. Even at their pace of a fast walk, Tag's raiders would be on the Soviets in less than ten minutes.

"Meat Grinder Three," Tag radioed back, "this is Butcher Boy. Request you drop back. Do not—I say again, do not—make contact. Over."

"Roger, Butcher Boy. Meat Grinder Three out."

But as Tag was drawing a long breath of relief that Jan hadn't tipped their hand, the quiet of the forest was shattered by one, two, then three heavy machine guns, followed by the booming echoes of a rapid-fire cannon in the woods ahead of them.

"Attack speed," Tag ordered, and the five vehicles moving on line accelerated in unison.

The flurry of gunfire ended as quickly as it began. Tag keyed the TacNet and called to Jan, "Meat Grinder Three, this is Butcher Boy. What is your status? Over."

"Butcher Boy, this is Grinder Three. Okay here. You have two targets moving to your left and two to the right, moving very fast. Over."

"Roger, Grinder Three. Hold your position and keep your ears open. Butcher Boy out."

Of all the considerations that flashed through

Tag's mind, none was more baffling to him than the shock of recognition that these Soviets were executing a fundamental textbook maneuver from the pages of Ross Kettle. He tried to shake it off. It had to be coincidence, blind luck. But . . .

"Meat Grinder One, Meat Grinder Two, this is Butcher Boy. Targets are splitting right and left. Don't let us lose them. Go now."

Giesla and Betcher acknowledged his command and wheeled their cars at right angles to the line of advance, spinning rooster tails of forest mulch from beneath their tires and flying past the Bradleys.

"Lazarus, Disciple," Tag radioed, using the call signs that Prentice and N. Sain had adopted, "this is Butcher Boy. Off-load your Alpha Tango cargo. Lazarus, take a bearing on ten o'clock. Disciple, take a bearing on two o'clock. Both of you, move out. Attack speed."

Prentice and N. Sain halted their APCs long enough to disgorge one Dragon team and one LAW-equipped fire team each, then sped into the forest in a diverging vee.

Tag assembled the foot troops hastily, outlined their mission, and pointed them into the woods. "Keep your ears open," he told them, "and come to the sound of the guns. If this works, we might just run Ivan right into your laps, so stay sharp. Stay up on your radios, too, and if you see them before we do, go ahead and take what they offer. But stay in touch."

The two antitank teams fanned out into the forest, the camouflaged figures quickly losing themselves among the trees.

"What's our drill, Cap'n?" Wheels asked.

"We stay put," Tag said.

"Ah, shit," Fruits bitched.

"Be cool, Fruit Loops," Ham told him. "We are the cheese, little brother. Am I right, Bossman?"

"Something like that," Tag said. "Remember that little stunt we pulled in Honduras, when we got hit from behind in those woods?"

"Yeah," Fruits moaned. "We had a fuggin' Sheridan shot right out from unner us."

"After that, Fruits," Tag went on, "when we peeled those boys in front of us off to either side and had them fall back in on the Pan Ams from the flanks. That's what I think these Ivans are up to here."

"Now where'd they learn somethin' like that?" Wheels mused aloud.

"Damned if I know, Wheelman," Tag replied. "It for shittin' sure didn't come out of their maneuvers manual, but if they show up, I don't want to disappoint 'em. We're the cheese, all right, the cheese in the trap. And if that doesn't work, we'll hunt 'em down and skin their sorry asses."

Ham Jefferson was the only one of Tag's crew who took a real interest in the art of tactics, and he was the only one besides Tag who guessed what was happening when they heard the percussive reports of a BMP's 73mm cannon coming from the direction of Prentice's Bradley.

"Oh, fuck my dead dog runnin'," Ham said tightly. "They got a goddamn stay-behind, Bossman. You were right."

Wheels revved the turbines. "Scoot and shoot?" he asked.

"No," Tag said. "Chuck will have to handle this one, Wheels. We can't leave the middle open. If they are running the pick-and-roll, they'll be back this way."

All that the crew of the XM-F4 could do was stay alert and try to judge the tide of the fight by the sounds of the guns.

The stay-behind ambush was one of several standard wrinkles in the maneuver that Tag slugged a pick-and-roll. Prentice's Bradley, with Sergeant White at the stick, was careening through the timber, trying to gauge the angle and cut off the fleeing enemy, when it was struck by a 73mm salvo from the cannon of a BMP. Calculating the approach, the BMP commander had dropped behind its companion tank and when he heard the Bradley rushed forward from cover to meet it. Only the slick-skin armor saved the American armored personnel carrier and the men inside.

The BMP had three rounds in the air before Prentice and his driver had recovered from the impact of the first, which struck high on the nose of the Bradley, midway between the prismatic view slits, spilling men from the back benches and whipping White and Prentice in their seats.

Prentice saw the muzzle-blast signatures on the Phalanx screen, jabbed at the lock in, and at the same time ordered White to juke left. One more round from the now-halted BMP raked the side armor of the Bradley as it executed its turn behind the cover of a stand of birch, and the ratcheting barrels of the Phalanx sawed their tops to dust. Only a handful of the 37mm slugs found the BMP through the trees, but their depleted-uranium cores tore fist-size holes in the armor of the Soviet APC, wounding two of the crew and sending the vehicle scooting for cover.

Prentice brought his Bradley from behind the birches just in time to see the BMP zigging away

from its ambush. "Get him," the young lieutenant said, grimacing in pain from his half-healed
dislocated shoulder, and White spun the turbine.
The souped-up Bradley was no match in speed or
agility for the No Slack Too, but it was a pit bull
against a puppy to the BMP. White closed the gap,
and in seconds Prentice was again catching blips
of their quarry on the target-acquisition screen.

The commander of the BMP was neither a coward nor a fool, but he did not realize what he
had encountered. He tried to keep the pursuing
Bradley at a distance by rotating his cannon to
the rear and slinging wild shots back along his
path. But Prentice had little fear of the 73mm,
after seeing the slick skin turn the initial hits,
and he pressed his driver forward, looking for an
open shot, while rounds from the BMP blasted
tree trunks and branches all around him.

At last, the Soviet commander realized that
he could run but he couldn't hide. Spotting a
giant walnut tree that grew in double trunks, he
wheeled his crippled BMP behind them and laid
his gun for a desperation shot at the relentless
Bradley on his tail.

The heavy stutter of the Phalanx's recoil was
thrumming through the frame of the Bradley as
it broke into the open, pouring a stream of fire
into the vee of the trees concealing the BMP. The
Soviet crew never got off a round. The continuous
skein of 37mm slugs split their lightly armored
APC from glacis to exhaust grille, and the explosion of its ammunition magazine peeled back the
halves like a rotten ruptured fruit.

"Bingo," Ham Jefferson announced, his ear
glued to the audiodirectional headset and his

eyes on the tracking screen. "Score one for the good guys, captain. Ol' Chuckles nailed him."

Tag, standing in his hatch, said, "I heard, Hambone. Is he still moving?"

Before Jefferson could reply, the TacNet popped on and Prentice came over the radio: "Butcher Boy, this is Lazarus. We have one dead Bravo Mike Poppa. Request instructions. Over."

"Lazarus, this is Butcher Boy," Tag answered. "Good shooting. Continue pursuit."

"Roger. Lazarus out."

As Tag and Prentice were breaking off their transmission, Giesla and her loader, Horst, caught their first sight of the compact tank that had split off with the ambushing BMP. Giesla had driven like a woman possessed to outspeed the Communist tank, slewing through the woods like a slalom skier, downshifting and accelerating and hardly touching her brakes, holding the three-liter Porsche engine near the redline, while Horst held white-knuckled to the brace bar on the dash. She heard the stay-behind ambush as it was sprung and the running fight between Prentice and the BMP, but she never slowed until she was confident that no 2S9-type tank, no matter what its modifications, could possibly have outdistanced her. Then, seeing a brush-covered step of high ground, she slung her gun buggy in a one-eighty turn and raced into the cover.

Giesla let the motor fall to an idle and lifted the gull-wing door on the crew cowl.

"Horst," she said, "arm the missiles," as she stepped halfway outside, one foot still in the car, straining her ears for sounds of motors or movement. She did not know what had happened in the fight that broke out behind her, but she had not heard the report of a heavy gun, such as the 120mm carried by the compact tank, so she had to assume that it was still somewhere in the forest.

In less than a minute, she heard it, first only a crashing sound and then the growl of a laboring diesel.

Giesla slid back in her seat, closed the gull wing, and opened the Plexiglas side curtain.

"Lock on target," she said quietly to Horst as she lifted the radio handset from its cradle.

"Butcher Boy, this is Meat Grinder One. I have visual contact with a Two-Sierra-Niner, approximately five-zero-zero meters south of last position. Do we engage? Over."

"Grinder One, this is Butcher Boy. Negative. Maintain visual contact and keep me posted, but do not engage unless he spots you. You copy? Over."

"Copy. Grinder One out."

Giesla replaced the handset roughly, frustrated by Tag's orders. She had wanted the tiny tank badly. At the same time, she was uneasy with their position. The Soviet tank was moving fast across her left front and would soon pass out of the target line of her missiles, no more than seventy-five meters away. She could see the commander standing in the turret, and she knew that any movement on her part, any attempt to shift position to keep her missiles and recoilless rifles trained on the tank, risked giving her away. The bushes were high and gave good concealment, but once the 2S9 was on her flank she would be utterly defenseless.

Giesla licked salt off her upper lip and said to Horst, "Breathe softly, soldier."

Horst swallowed and did as he was told.

She had no fear of the Soviet tanker hearing her idling engine over the noise of his own, but Giesla could hardly bring herself to move her head to keep the passing tank in sight, fearing that any movement might catch the enemy's eye. As the tank passed out of the corner of her vision without seeing the gun vehicle and she began to quell her pulse, a change in the pitch of the tank's engine caused the adrenaline to start to flow again: it was turning, circling back on them.

Without haste, Giesla reached up and opened the hatch in the roof of the crew cowl that gave access to the .50-caliber mounted on the external roll cage. She shed her helmet, stood, and looked back over the exhaust stacks. To her relief, she saw the Communist tank making a wide swing around her position until it was headed back north.

Giesla dropped back in her seat and snatched up the radio.

"Butcher Boy, this is Grinder One. The Two-Sierra-Niner has turned and is heading toward your position. Request instructions. Over."

"Grinder One, this is Butcher Boy. Roger your last. Come in behind target and maintain a one-zero-zero meter interval. Over."

"Roger, Butcher Boy. Grinder One out."

Now, Tag thought, *now we've got him.* He radioed Prentice and the Rangers on the ground to get them into position, then had Wheels reposition the No Slack Too to face the approach of the 2S9, all the while trying to ignore the thunder of a cannon and the sporadic hammering of a Phalanx gun off to his right flank.

•   •   •

To the north of Tag's position, the woods were less cut over, the undergrowth and saplings denser, so Sergeant Betcher, with Karl as his driver, had to make a wide loop to get ahead of the BMP and the 2S9 that had broken in that direction, and N. Sain's Bradley had had similar problems trying to quarter on the Soviets' path. So, when Betcher did at last see the enemy armor, it was far from N. Sain or the Rangers and in a bad place to fight, a stand of overgrown forest where it was next to impossible to get a shot of more than fifty meters.

Thinking that N. Sain was closing from the rear, Betcher laid his recoilless rifles along a limb-clotted alley through the woods and fired two tubes as the 2S9 crossed it. One of the 106mm projectiles caromed off a larch and detonated in the treetops, and the second just clipped the leading edge of the compact tank, peeling back a track skirt, but leaving the tank otherwise intact.

Karl gunned the engine, and their car shot into the woods as a hail of machine-gun fire raked the place where they had been.

The confused tankers first accelerated blindly on an interception course with Betcher's gun buggy. Then, as the Jagd Kommandos were coming around for another shot, the 2S9 suddenly turned back on its path, radioing to its companion BMP to do the same.

Following the command, the Soviet armored personnel carrier was in the middle of a 120-degree turn when it practically collided with N. Sain's Bradley crashing through a brake of saplings. The two APCs sprayed each other with ineffectual machine-gun fire at point-blank range as they both jockeyed for a position where they could bring their heavier weapons to bear, like two mastiffs working for the throat. Despite its lively turbine engine and N. Sain's maniacal driving, the Bradley full of Rangers was too heavy to outmaneuver the BMP, which broke contact and lost itself in the stand of saplings that N. Sain had just broken through.

The Disciple of Darkness managed to jerk the Bradley into a stationary fighting position, nose toward the BMP, but had no chance for a shot from the clearing the size of a basketball court that the two APCs had wallowed in the undergrowth.

"Curses of Kali," N. Sain roared, triggering a Phalanx burst in frustration. "Make the ballast walk. We got to shake and bake, run with the hooligan wind. Out. Out."

Rabies dropped the troop ramp, and Gaylord Krager looked at Sergeant Dunn, the squad leader.

"You know, Dunn," Krager said, "the crazy sonofabitch is right. Let's hunt." Rangers were still piling off the ramp when N. Sain hit the throttle.

A half kilometer farther south, Tag was drawing tight his noose on the lone 2S9. Prentice had put the remainder of his Rangers on the ground and moved his Bradley closer to the Communist tank's projected route; Giesla continued to stalk from the rear; and Tag now had a solid audiodirectional fix on their prey.

"Wolfman," Tag radioed to Villalobos, squad leader for the Rangers in Prentice's APC, "move your pack one-zero-zero meters east and set up Alpha Tango positions. You copy? Over."

"Wolfman copy."

"Butcher Boy out."

During the next thirty seconds, things seemed to happen all at once. The 2S9 veered from its head-on course toward the No Slack Too, angling slightly to Tag's right. Even before he could relay the change to Prentice, an ATGM sizzled from the Bradley's racks and detonated against a thick fir in a shower of flaming needles. The Soviet commander launched a tube-fired missile as he turned, blasting a crater the size of a German sedan at the feet of the American APC. Tag triggered a swarm of 37mm from the Phalanx into the area indicated on his audiodirectional scope, hoping a few stray rounds might find their way through the scrub and trees. A fire team of Rangers released a pair of LAWs as the 2S9 came into their field of fire at long range, one flying wild and the other delivering a crunching explosion to the tank's turret, jamming it and killing the gunner inside. The commander turned away from the fire, retreating at full speed back to the south and directly into the flame-tipped muzzles of Giesla's recoilless rifles. At seventy-five meters and closing, her 106mm high-explosive rounds both found the mark, striking the 2S9's glacis inside each track fender and collapsing it like punched bread dough, smoke billowing in place of flour. The compact tank stopped so short that its tracks came off the ground in the rear and crashed down again on dead shocks.

Within the minute it took Tag and the No Slack Too to cover the distance to the burning tank, Giesla, Prentice, and the first of Villalobos's Ranger squad were already there. In another minute, the squad was back in the Bradley, and all three vehicles were fanning out to fall on the Soviet armor sparring with Betcher and N. Sain.

"All units, all units," Tag radioed as they ran, "this is Butcher Boy. Get us prisoners, if you can. I say again, prisoners. Butcher Boy out."

N. Sain and Betcher heard the transmission, the first ignoring it and the other unable to give it serious thought. N. Sain was tearing furious divots from the forest floor as he jinked through the second growth in single-minded pursuit of the BMP, and Betcher was busy dodging machine-gun fire from the skittering tank, as each tried to gain an advantage in the thick timber and unlimber the heavy guns.

The commander of the remaining Soviet tank heard the radio chatter as well, and while he spoke no English, he knew there were too many voices on the air for him to think the pick-and-roll might work. Not really trusting what he had learned from his regimental commander's briefings on Kettle's tactics, he saw no recourse but to attempt a breakout. He suddenly turned from his parallel track with Betcher and cut for the open forest to the south, bursting into the middle of Tag's formation, fifty meters from the No Slack Too.

Ham Jefferson fired on reflex, striking the 2S9 broadside. At that range, the 120mm HE round carried through the crew compartment and exited in an explosion that opened the whole side of the tank, splattering the woods with shrapnel and savaged body parts.

"Splish-splash, Mister Jefferson," Tag said. "Nice shot. Wheels, home in on those guns."

Followed by Prentice's Bradley and the two Kommando cars, the No Slack Too charged toward the running duel between N. Sain and the remaining BMP. Betcher picked them up and fell into the formation, and Krager radioed to say that his Rangers were enveloping on the Soviet personnel carrier.

Tag wanted prisoners. "Disciple, this is Butcher Boy. Break contact. I say again, break contact. Do you copy? Over."

Nothing.

Tag banged the side of his helmet. "Disciple, Disciple, this is Butcher Boy. Do you read me? Over."

N. Sain's voice came back soft and dreamy. "I read, I heed, o Avatar of Ambush. But the beat goes on."

The exchange of Phalanx and cannon rounds did not slacken, and Tag pushed his driver to close on the fight. Wheels did all he could, slinging the thirty-ton tank through a series of switchbacks in the heavy timber. When Tag at last saw the sparring APCs, the Soviet was running east, shielded from N. Sain's gun by a wooded swale thick with young larch. Tag took the Phalanx and aimed for the treads on the BMP. His second burst disintegrated the right-rear drive cog and carrier assembly, bringing the BMP to a shuddering halt, as smoke began to pour out of its rear grille and men out of its hatches.

The Soviet crew was lucky. Stumbling, coughing, half blinded by the smoke, they were less than fifty meters from their vehicle when N. Sain cleared the stand of larch and lashed out with a gout of fire from the Phalanx, setting off a string of secondary explosions inside the BMP that blasted black-tipped flames through every hole and fissure in the armor plate. Oily smoke enveloped the BMP and rose in a thick coil through the tree tops.

Within minutes, the Rangers had fanned out and collected the three stunned Soviet soldiers, loaded them in Prentice's Bradley, mounted up, and were speeding back to the south behind the No Slack Too.

Five kilometers to the southwest, the woods ended at a road that marked the beginning of the small dairy farms, orchards, and vineyards that covered most of the countryside from here to Lake Constance. An abandoned farm straddled the road, with buildings on either side, and here Tag elected to set up his rear area, where the Jagd Kommandos would be staged as a quick-reaction force to cover the outer margin of the radioactive zone, while the No Slack Too and the Bradleys patrolled inside it. The Rangers threw up a defensive perimeter around two barns that sat between the woods and the road, and Tag assembled Giesla, Prentice, Krager, and his crew, along with the three prisoners, in one of them.

It had been a long morning, and as everyone's adrenaline wore off, they turned ravenously hungry. Tag leaned back with his elbows on the possibles box of Giesla's Kommando car, noisily chewing a mouthful of apple and cheese and mugging playfully at the three prisoners sitting bound on the floor of the barn.

He said to Giesla, who was perched on one of the honeycomb rear tires, "Any idea who these guys are, their unit, I mean?"

"Some unit of the First Guards, I think, from the markings on their vehicles. Maybe the anti-tank regiment. But they look lost and hungry to me."

"Gaylord," Tag said to Krager, who had been getting the Grand Tour of the No Slack Too from

Wheels Latta, "you think these boys are hungry?"

"I think you could get a scrap up among 'em over that apple core," Krager said as he walked over from the tank. "You give 'em just a little food and no water, and in forty-eight hours they'll tell me anything I want about each other."

Tag said, "You are one evil sonofabitch, Gaylord, and I wish we had time for you to prove it, but we've got to get what we can out of these boys right now. We're going to be moving again, no later than fourteen-hundred hours."

N. Sain, barefoot and wearing only a filthy pair of fatigue trousers, padded down the length of the barn from where his Bradley was parked, his arms flapping like broken wings. He stopped, facing Tag and Krager, twitched, and said, "My Guide, my Teacher, Seer of the Beast's belly, can I play with them?" He pointed at the prisoners, who momentarily forgot their fear and hunger and sat staring in incredulity at the flapping gestures and disparate voices that were Sergeant M. N. Sain, U.S. Army Reserve.

Tag shook his head. "Not a chance," he said. "You are some kind of asshole disciple, my friend. If you had been in true harmony with the Dark Design, we wouldn't have them here in the first place. But your karma was shit because you wouldn't listen. We deal death, it is our instrument, and we do not sow it broadcast and cheapen it by pointless repetition. Some, Disciple, do not deserve it."

N. Sain bobbed his head and shoulders to some rhythm that none of the others could hear and smiled rapturously at Tag. "Fear-fucking beautiful," he said as he turned away and moon-walked back to his Bradley, where the muffled wailing of "All Along The Watch Tower" could be heard leaking through the hatches.

Krager shook his head, muttered, "A goddamn original," then turned to Tag and said, "So how do we get our little friends involved in show-and-tell?"

"You may like this, Gaylord," Tag said. "Giesla, are you ready?"

She slid off the tire, brushed crumbs from her jumpsuit, and joined the men at the rear of the car. "Is your Mister Jefferson available?" she asked Tag.

Tag nodded. "He should be. Ham," he shouted, "come over here, and bring your powers of persuasion with you."

Giesla upended a milk bucket and sat down on it, facing the prisoners. She spoke to them casually in Russian and got a *da* and two *nyets* in reply. Her voice took a harder edge, and when one of the soldiers began to talk, another kicked him and spoke harshly.

Ham Jefferson appeared about that time, *tsk*ing his tongue and saying, "Manners, manners. I think we oughta let 'em talk to us one at a time, if that's the way they're gonna be."

Giesla agreed and ordered Jan to take two of them off. Ham found another bucket for himself and a milking stool for the Russian soldier. Ham helped him onto the stool, drew his own bucket up beside, flicked a slender fighting knife with an eight-inch blade out of his jumpsuit, and sat down staring at the side of the Russian soldier's head, less than a foot away. Ham made soft kissing sounds.

Giesla barked at the prisoner, who cut his eyes toward her and away from Ham. She asked him a question; he shook his head and said a few words. She asked another and another and each time got the same sort of response. She rose, still speaking, and nodded to Ham.

Ham ran his free hand softly across the top of the Russian's head and down to the nape of his neck, where he locked on with long, strong fingers. He raised the knife, lay it flat against the Russian's far cheek, just beneath his eye, then leaned forward and planted a hard, wet kiss on his jaw. The soldier's eyes widened in three kinds of fear, and he was babbling to Giesla before she finished her question.

She let him run on for a while before she gave Ham the eye, and he released the trembling prisoner. She was getting answers now, and she pumped the soldier for fifteen minutes before she was satisfied that he had told her all he knew. Without stopping to translate, she called for the next prisoner, and she and Ham repeated variations on their good-cop-bad-cop technique. When she was finished with the third, she rose off the pail and rejoined Tag and Krager at the back of her vehicle. Ham followed her, and she kissed him full on the mouth.

"Now, that," Ham said as he stepped back, "is what I call fraternization. Uh-huh, a court-martial offense if ever I saw one."

"I did not want Master Sergeant Krager to get the wrong impression of you," she said with a smile.

Krager extended his hand to her. "Ma'am," he said, "you and Jefferson have nothing but my respect and admiration. But tell me, *would* you have kissed him on the mouth, Jefferson?"

"With all respect due, in yo ofay ear, Master Sergeant," said Ham.

"Oh dear," Krager said, bringing his fingertips to his mouth, "even worse than I feared."

"Giesla," Tag said, "break it down for us. What did these guys have to say?"

"Not a lot, I am afraid. They were part of the security for the nuclear convoy—part of the decoy detachment, actually—and they have been cut off themselves these past days. As we suspected, they are with the antitank regiment of the First Guards, a Colonel Yeshev commanding."

The name rang a distant bell in Tag's memory. "And that's it? That's all we get for an hour of interrogation?"

"Not quite," Giesla said. "Apparently their captain, who died in one of the 2S9s we encountered this morning, received at least a fragment of a transmission earlier and had ordered them toward a village called Grabbe, where they were heading when we found them."

"Well," Tag said, "I guess that makes it easy. Don't you, Gaylord?"

Krager nodded. "Grabbe it and growl, I say."

5

The Rangers in their tree-bark camouflaged NBC suits milled around the No Slack Too and the Bradleys, looking grim and apprehensive, nervously checking their weapons and fingering the NBC accessories on their combat harnesses—gas masks, air filters, decontamination kits. A few of them had been pressed into service to help Mad Dog, Rabies, and the men of Tag's crew as they readied the armor for the radiation zone. A resupply drone had dropped fuel cells in for them shortly after noon, and while the vehicles were being filled, Tag had the men double-check all of the NBC defenses, secure the synthetic-rubber boots on the gun mantles, and review the procedures in case of accidental contamination, including the use of the patch kits designed to seal holes in the slick-skin armor.

"Why is it," Ham Jefferson mused as he ticked off the patch kits on his checklist, "that I don't feel good about having those things with us?"

"Is kinda like wishing for bad luck and knocking on wood, ain't it?" Wheels said, shutting the No Slack Too's toolbox and latching the lid. "But like my granny used to say about saving bottles, 'You never know when it might rain whiskey.'"

"Yeah?" Fruits sneered. "And did it?"

"Not yet, Fruit Loops," Wheels said, grinning. "But that don't mean it won't. Granny said that, too."

Tag, finished with the final inspection of the Rangers, walked up with Giesla, Prentice, Krager, and N. Sain and said, "Last call, sweethearts. Hit the latrine, if you need to. We're pulling out in fifteen minutes."

"Ah," said Ham, putting aside his clipboard, "a good commander thinks of all the details," and he ambled off with Wheels and Fruits.

Tag climbed in his hatch, took his seat at the command console, and pivoted the VLD screen down into place. With the others crowded around the open hatch, he began to call up details of the area between their position and the village of Grabbe, overlaying the topography with satellite and recon photos, including the infrared and radar images, until he had the composite elements he needed. He pressed the key for printouts, and the multicolor printer began to whir and hiss. In minutes, he had corrected maps showing every physical detail and the intensity of every irradiated acre between the Danube and Lake Constance. He pushed himself up and out of the hatch and handed the maps to Giesla, Prentice, Krager, and N. Sain.

"Giesla," he said, "we don't really know what communications will be like once we're inside the zone, so I want you to spread your three cars far enough apart along the perimeter to get a triangulation. That may be the only way you have of keeping track of us. Keep a close watch on your six, too; it's likely that Ivan still has some strays wandering around. You want a couple of fire teams for security?"

Giesla shook her head. "No, Max," she said. "We have no way to carry them; they would only slow us down." Her face was heavy with concern.

"Okay, then," Tag resumed, "everybody, look at your maps. If we had gone around the north end of these woods, we could have had an open corridor to this northern route into Grabbe. As it is, I think we'll do as well to continue as planned and pick our way in from here. Now, I want all of you to remember that our primary mission is reconnaissance, but I know for a fact that Kettle wants the First Guards punished. So we don't pass up any chances to spank 'em. We'll stick to this road as far west as we can, but we will have to swing wide around these hot spots here"—he tapped a string of angry red blotches on the map—"and then just see what the actual radiation levels add up to in the seams between the fallout zones."

"What's our formation?" Prentice asked.

"Close," said Tag. "I couldn't detail them on the VLD, but those yellow zones have measles, hundreds of small hot spots, from debris, I guess. We damn sure don't need one of you picking up a hot rock in a tread. You watch your cumulative RAD levels. We're not going to have anybody getting fried."

He paused and looked at the crescent of expressionless faces. "Any questions?"

Five minutes later, the No Slack Too rolled west toward the atomic strike zone, with the two Bradleys full of Rangers behind, moving fast on the crown of the three-lane farm highway that once had run to Grabbe. All three vehicles were tightly buttoned, with all their NBC defenses in place, every sensor fine-tuned to detect radio-active nuance. Soon, their oscilloscreens were recording low domes of radiation, then quick, brief spikes that never quite fell back to their initial level, and the ambient RAD count rose steadily.

"Jeez," Fruits said, looking down from the turret over Tag's shoulder at the screen, "it's really gettin' warm out dere, Captain Max."

Ham Jefferson, in his gunner's chair on the other side of the 120mm, pointed to the radiation counter on the inside of the hatch and said, "But we be cool, Tutti Fruity."

Wheels spoke over the intercom: "Relax, Fruits. Take the cob out and enjoy the ride, son. Hell, the air in New York is worse than this."

No, Tag thought, it wasn't. Through his prismatic periscope he could see plainly the effects of even the relatively small doses of fallout that had blanketed the immediate area. He saw the curled grass in the meadows and the withered wildflowers in the fencerows. Poisoned livestock lay down in the fields, already sick with the atomic toxins, and no birds flew in the sky.

As the small column approached the concentration of nuclear impacts where they would have to leave the road, Tag slowed their pace and studied the map, noting two avenues they might take, depending upon how close to ground zero they could actually come before having to make their detour. As they topped a high rise, the sensors spiked, and Tag called a halt. He increased the magnification of his commander's scope and panned across the distance.

Still more than five kilometers from the nearest ground zero, he could not mistake the air-burst signatures of tactical nukes. At this distance there was little detail he could make out—indeed, there was little detail left above ground level on the rolling plateau—only a dark smudge striated with charred, flattened trees and pimpled here and there with ruined walls left standing by some freak of physics. Tag guessed that the ionization radius—the distance from an atomic blast in which virtually everything is either blown to dust or vitrified—was a kilometer or more, and that where they now were represented the limit of the tactical envelope, where up to eighty percent of the exposed and unprotected might likely survive the initial explosion. Yet even here, immediately in front of him and no more than two-hundred meters away, he could see flattened outbuildings and fruit trees stripped of their limbs. He glanced down at the RAD counter.

"Lazarus, Disciple," Tag radioed, "this is Butcher Boy. Close up and follow me." Then over the intercom he said, "Wheels, bend us back due north, as best you can, and guide left at my command."

"You got it, Cap'n," Wheels said as he turned to his right along the top of the rise, rode down a wire fence, and led the Bradleys across an open meadow.

This was good country for tankers trained in Ross Kettle's tactics—mostly open and rolling, with enough roads, farmsteads, and villages to provide excellent mobility and a variety of cover. It gave Tag something to like about their situation.

As the radiation count dropped on Tag's screen, he had Wheels correct their course back to the west by small degrees. They crossed secondary roads, forded streams, and clattered over the cobbled streets of empty villages, seeing only the occasional stray animal lurching and bawling in agony. Tag refused to let his men put them down, but it was some of the hardest fire discipline he ever had to enforce. The staggering hogs and horses and the cattle terrified by their own pain were pitiful to even the most callused veteran, but nothing was worth the risk of giving themselves away by a mercy slaughter.

Judging by the damage to some of the area by conventional weaponry—the shell-pocked roads and bombed-out buildings—Tag reckoned that, as intelligence had assured him, most of the civilian population had abandoned the region during the opening assault, fleeing before the Soviets' armored blitz or dying in the cross fire of the opposing armies. But as he guided his patrol around the north rim of the radiation zone, it became equally clear that there were pockets that had been spared by both the initial attack and the nuclear exchange. In fact, as he was discovering, there were seams of almost normal radiation levels that the satellite images had not been able to distinguish, in addition to the relatively broad corridor between the line of Soviet bombardment and the Allied counter strikes.

Nearing the wooded outskirts of a market town that had once been home to some twenty-thousand souls, Tag realized that the tiny blip of green on his map was actually much larger than indicated, for the radiation levels had hovered at the high end of normal range for more than two kilometers. He stopped at the top of the gentle slope of woods that overlooked the town, its broad valley, and small river, bemused by the peaceful panorama that lay spread before him like a scene on a picture postcard. Despite being the economic hub of the agricultural valley and being located at a major crossroads, Badenthaler was not itself a strategic necessity for either army. It had no commanding terrain, no military garrison or other installation, and no particular military significance, save that it needed to be secured for transit, and the single rail spur that served it had been taken out by Jagd Kommandos long before the Soviet advance reached here.

Scanning the town and the valley with his scope, Tag saw movement and thin wisps of chimney smoke.

"Wheels," he said, "stop here and give me a reading off the skin."

Wheels brought them to a halt on the unimproved road they had been following and said to Tag, "Looks clean, Cap'n, but the treads are prob'ly a little dirty, maybe the edges of the fenders."

"Good enough," said Tag, unbuckling from his seat and taking his day/night binoculars from their cubbyhole. "We've got activity down there in—what's it?—Badenthaler. You radio Prentice and N. Sain. I'm going to put the top down and try to get a better look. Coming through." And he hauled himself up into the turret and threw back the hatch.

From the top of the tank, Tag had a better angle and a wider field of vision than his commander's scope provided, and he could see that while there was smoke from flues and chimneys in several parts of town, the only activity he could determine was confined to an area around the rail terminal at one end of the village, near the loading docks and squat concrete grain elevator. As he studied the layout and tried to figure out what was happening, a brief exchange of small-arms fire told him that the war had not passed the town by entirely. From the sound of the reports, however, it did not sound like a military engagement, at least not like an exchange between two military units. The ragged rattle of gunfire that began the flurry was not coming from automatic weapons or from weapons of the same caliber, although the return fire had the distinctive chop of full-auto AKs, but not many of them. Tag glimpsed figures darting among firing positions surrounding the grain silo, none of them in uniform.

Tag dropped back through the turret and into his seat.

"What's the skinny?" Ham Jefferson asked.

"Looks like the locals have got some bad guys bottled up in a grain silo down by the railroad tracks," Tag said. "Fruits, load HE."

While the carousel spun the high-explosive round into the 120mm, Tag studied his map, then keyed the TacNet.

"Lazarus, this is Butcher Boy. We have some small-arms action in the vil down below, around the grain elevator by the tracks. Looks like Ivan is in the silo, holding off the locals. I want you to envelop on them from the north and hold a blocking position, while we go in and take them out. You copy? Over."

"Roger, Butcher Boy," Prentice replied. "Ten minutes. Over."

"Roger, Lazarus. One-zero minutes. And remember: we're taking prisoners. Butcher Boy out."

As Prentice's Bradley shot past, Tag called to N. Sain: "Disciple, this is Butcher Boy. Did you monitor my last? Over."

"Most intensely," N. Sain replied, ever oblivious to radio procedure.

"Roger, Disciple. I want you to cover our six and be ready to put Blade Runner and his people on the ground. You copy? Over."

"Like singing knives, like singing knives, o Avatar. Yes, we will."

N. Sain broke the transmission abruptly, and Tag could only shake his head.

"Okay," he said to his crew, "let's start crawling. Wheels, give Prentice plenty of time."

"Through the woods, Cap'n?" Wheels asked.

"Right, Wheelman. No point in letting anybody know we're here until they need to. Go."

The No Slack Too, with N. Sain pulling up the rear, quartered down the face of the slope at an angle that would take them around the center of town and onto a paved road that ran directly to the silo and the surrounding warehouses. Once there, Tag intended to run full tilt for their target, before the Soviets inside could react. With any luck, some of them would flush and be picked up by Villalobos's Ranger squad. It would be Ivan's worse luck if they decided to stand and fight.

Wheels took his time, making it easy for the trailing Bradley to negotiate the rocky watercourses that they had to cross. Tag halted them again at the edge of the woods by the road and went up top for a last look. From here he could not see the base of the silo for the cluster of warehouses, but he could see a group of men gathered behind one of them, all holding long-barreled sporting rifles. Tag disappeared back inside and into his seat.

"Lazarus," Tag said over the TacNet, "this is Butcher Boy. Are you in position? Over."

"Affirmative, Butcher Boy," Prentice replied. "Over."

"Stand to, Lazarus. We're going in. Butcher Boy out."

"What's shakin', Bossman?" Ham asked.

"About what I thought," Tag said. "There's some civilians with hunting rifles out behind one of the storage buildings, and I don't think who-ever's in the silo can see over it. Let's take it slow going in, Wheels, so we don't spook the locals."

"All ahead slow," Wheels said, engaging the transmission.

The No Slack Too crossed the ditch between the woods and the road and rolled down the last half kilometer toward the desultory firefight. Tag kept his eyes glued to the periscope and suffered a moment of confusion when he saw the civilians behind the building scatter and, moments later, heard rifle shots pinging off the slick-skin armor.

"Fuck, shit," Fruits Tutti sputtered, "de bastids are shootin' at us, Captain Max."

Tag was on the TacNet immediately. "Disciple, Disciple, this is Butcher Boy. Ignore the incoming. I say again, ignore the incoming. It's friendly fire. Do you copy? Over."

"It is all friendly," N. Sain replied, letting the air go dead.

"Stand easy," Tag said to his crew. "Hell, they think we're Ivan. Wheels, Ham, let's show 'em our colors. Run and gun."

The twin turbines on the No Slack Too spun, and chunks of asphalt flew from beneath the treads as Wheels cocked open the throttles. The XM-F4 was topping one hundred kilometers per hour when it came into the flats around the rail terminus and screamed across the concrete apron

of the loading docks. Everywhere Tag turned his
scope, he could see civilians bailing out of their
firing positions among the produce trucks and
empty boxcars. Wheels rounded the corner of the
warehouse where Tag had first seen the men
with the rifles, and Tag's first target filled the
eyepiece on his scope. There was no mistaking
the bullet pocks that marred the finished concrete
around the windows of a square, ground-level
annex attached to the base of the silo.

Tag centered his scope on the ell. "Target."

"Confirmed," Ham replied coolly.

"Shoot."

"Shot."

From less than one hundred meters away, the
impact of the 120mm seemed instantaneous, ripping a hole the size of a car in the wall and sending windows, doors, and roof flying outward in a
shower of shards and dust that totally blanketed
what was left of the business office of the grain
elevator. The remains of the half-dozen Soviet
soldiers inside were practically indistinguishable
from the rest of the debris.

"Keep it up, Wheels," Tag said as the loading carousel whirled another HE round into the
breech of the main tube. "Let's see what we got
on the other side."

The No Slack Too hammered over the main
rail spur and the siding that ran to the elevator, swinging wide to give Ham an angle
on whatever was behind it. On the side of
the silo away from the tracks was a complex of sheds, scales, and grain augers where
the remainder of the Soviet soldiers had bar-
ricaded themselves, and Tag saw at once that
several had decamped and were running for the

cover of the locomotive shop at the end of the line.

Engaging the Phalanx himself, Tag raked the sheet metal and fertilizer sacks of the Soviets' makeshift parapets, bringing down the augers and conveyer chutes in a tangle of twisted parts. The depleted-uranium slugs pulverized men, concrete, and metal in an earsplitting wave of explosions that left the surviving Soviet soldiers huddled in terror beneath the rubble of their redoubt. It all took less than ten seconds.

"Square up on the target, Wheels," Tag told his driver, "and hold your position."

Wheels brought the No Slack Too around and stopped, facing the ruin on the side of the silo. Through his scope, Tag could see dead and wounded sprawled among the wreckage.

"Cover me," he said, and he shinnied up into the turret and out the hatch. He swung the naval-mounted mini gun into position and called out, "Surrender. Come out of there and give it up. Now." He doubted that any of the Soviet soldiers who had not been temporarily deafened by the Phalanx could speak English, but he imagined that they would get the idea.

N. Sain had brought his Bradley up into position off the No Slack Too's left rear, and Tag radioed him to put Krager's Rangers out to sweep the Soviet position. At the same time, he heard automatic rifle fire from beyond the locomotive shop, followed by indistinct shouts as the shooting ceased.

The Rangers encircled the smoking remains of the Soviet position and advanced on it in team rushes, drawing no fire and quickly overrunning the barricades. They soon began herding out the survivors who could walk and carrying the rest, and in minutes they were joined by Villalobos's squad and another four dispirited Soviets, followed closely by Prentice's Bradley. By the time Tag had reassembled his raiders and their eleven prisoners, the local residents, guns still held at the ready, began to approach them from the trucks and boxcars and storage buildings surrounding the silo.

From the turret, Tag waved and shouted, "We're friends, Americans."

One of the civilians motioned to the others and came forward alone.

"Hello," he called to Tag in heavily accented English, "you are who?"

Tag removed his helmet and pushed back his hair with a professional soldier's self-consciousness of needing it cut. "Sir," he said, speaking slowly and clearly, "I am Captain Max Tag, United States Army, and these are my men." He swept his arm to take in the assembled raiders. "I am sorry if we surprised you."

The man's expression did not change, but he nodded and kept coming forward until he was ten feet from the rear of the tank. He was a large man of perhaps fifty, dressed in soiled city clothes and carrying an H&K semiautomatic sporting rifle. He had the carriage and demeanor of a man who is comfortable with responsibility, if not with humor. "I," he said, "am Herr Goethe, the mayor of Badenthaler. You will please to come down."

"Happy to," Tag said. He pushed himself up and out of the hatch and clambered down the side over the scalloped farings of the War Club missile racks, careful to jump clear of the track fenders in case the treads had thrown up any radioactive soil on them.

Tag approached Herr Goethe and extended his hand, which Goethe took in a hard, dry grip.

"I welcome you, Captain Tag," the mayor said. "You can, perhaps, tell us what is happening in this war."

"A little," said Tag. "And there may be much that you can tell us also."

A shot rang out, and dirt flew at Tag's and Goethe's feet. Tag grabbed the German and jerked him to the ground behind the No Slack Too. N. Sain's Phalanx erupted, and high on the side of the silo a section of concrete around an access opening disintegrated in a shower of dust.

"Gaylord," Tag shouted to Krager, "get some people up there ASAP." He turned to Goethe and said, "Is there a way up there from inside?"

"*Ja,*" Goethe replied, "a—what?—a ladder."

Krager and four men sprinted for the silo, while the rest of the Rangers and their prisoners, along with the armed civilians, bolted for cover.

They had to wait only a minute before Krager and his men returned, two of them carrying the shattered, lifeless form of a Soviet soldier with a radio on his back.

"Well," Krager said as he walked over to Tag and Goethe, "we didn't have to go far for that one. Your original blew him right through the interior wall, must have broken every bone in his body."

Tag nodded. The dead man's radio was the only one he had seen among the prisoners, and he wondered whether any of this little set-to had been broadcast and to whom. But since there was nothing he could do if it had, he turned and said to Goethe, "Perhaps we should find a better place to talk, Herr Mayor."

"Yes," said Goethe. "Please, one minute."

He called to some of the townsmen nearest to them, and they came from their cover and poured over the smoking Soviet positions, picking up weapons and ammunition.

He turned back to Tag and said, "Come. Bring those prisoners. We have a place for them."

Idling along at a walking pace, the No Slack Too and the Bradleys followed Goethe, Tag, the Rangers, and the prisoners through the streets of town, between mixed blocks of 17th-century houses and modern apartment and commercial buildings, to the municipal complex on the square, where Goethe ordered the prisoners into the city jail and invited Tag and his commanders into his office on the second story of a baroque building whose stairwells spiraled up toward domed ceilings in ornate witches' nests.

Tag, Prentice, and Krager felt distinctly out of place in the high-ceilinged office, with its heavy oak furniture and marble floors covered in tapestry carpets. Goethe offered them coffee and sat behind his massive desk with the incongruous (and currently useless) computer at one end. He took a sip of his coffee, seeming in no hurry now that they were back in his familiar surroundings, and waited until they were all settled before he said, "How bad, Captain? What of my country is left?"

"You already know most of the worst, Herr Goethe, but it is over. The war is not over, but the Soviets are beaten, and there will be no more atomic war. I think. For now, you and your town are safe, but soon you will all have to leave. Everything around you is very bad, very radioactive. But tell me, what has happened here? Do you know who those soldiers were, where they came from?"

Goethe shook his head. Haltingly, he told Tag the story of the war in his town.

On the third day, Jagd Kommandos had arrived and destroyed the road and rail bridges, and the next day a Soviet armored column passed through, leaving only a small garrison to hold the town. The Kommandos attacked the rear of the column but were lost in doing it. A few days later, even the garrison withdrew. When they did, Goethe had organized a militia of police and civilians. The Soviets had destroyed the telephone offices and all the radios and transmitters they could find, including the commercial broadcast tower, so no one knew what the situation was beyond a few kilometers from town. A few men had tried to get away in cars or on motorcycles, but they never returned. When the nuclear exchange took place, everyone in the town thought it was the end, at first. And when they survived, many felt they were the only ones. Two days ago, a Soviet patrol had sneaked in past the militia sentries and tried to steal vehicles off the streets. The militia was able to assemble and drive them to the outskirts, where they occupied the grain elevators. Without heavy weapons, all the militia could do was keep them there with rifle fire and wait for them to starve. And that was what they had been doing when Tag and his raiders arrived. Goethe apologized for shooting at them, but how was he to know who they were. After all, their dull-black armor had no markings.

Tag waved off the apology. "No harm, no foul, Herr Goethe," he said. "When we have finished our mission, I will arrange to have everyone here evacuated. In the meanwhile, is there anything we can do for you? I do not want to stay here long, for that might bring more Soviets, but we will do what we can."

"No, captain ," Goethe replied. "We have food and good water in our tower. With rationing, we will be good for maybe three or four week, maybe more. Us you have helped. Tonight, you stay here. Talk to the prisoners and let us help you to food and beer. *Ja!*"

Tag thought a moment. The prisoners did need to be interrogated, and there was probably more to be learned from some of the townspeople. They could top their tanks from whatever fuel there was around, even if they had to siphon the cars, and take some pressure off their resupply.

"Ya," Tag said. "Yes. And we thank you. But tell me, is there anyone here who can speak Russian and English or even Russian? We need a good translator."

Goethe nodded. "One of our teachers from the school I think can. Him I will get."

"Good," said Tag. "We need to know all we can about what Ivan is up to."

Goethe looked puzzled at Tag's idiom, but again nodded, and they all rose to leave. Tag was, for the moment at least, feeling better about what they were doing. But he was nagged by uncertainty about what the Soviets were doing and where.

Yeshev was furious, furious and knotted with frustration. Still more than twenty-five kilometers from Grabbe, his column was stalled. After getting only six of his 2S9s across a rickety bridge that spanned a steep river gorge, his own T-8OB had proved too much for the structure, and he had been very lucky to be able to back off before the thing went down. Now, with the rest of his

compact tanks and all the T-8Os, he was stuck
on the wrong side, with no engineers and little
room to maneuver outside the clean path he had
picked for his approach to the town. Somewhere
out there he had a lost patrol with intelligence
that he needed badly, and somewhere else there
was that very dangerous contingent of armored
raiders he hoped to find and destroy.

As if all this were not enough, while studying
his maps and plotting recon routes for the BMPs
to help him find a way across the river, he received
the fragmented message that the sniper in the
silo had broadcast just before opening fire on Tag
and Goethe and being blasted from his perch by
N. Sain's Phalanx. For his political protection,
Yeshev had ordered one of his radio specialists
to make recordings of all radio traffic, and the
man was now trying to separate as much of the
message as he could from the background static
and distortion caused by electromagnetic inter-
ference acting on a weak signal. But what he had
gleaned so far was definitely not good.

Although his technician had been able to deci-
pher the call sign from the transmission, it was
not one familiar to Yeshev, beyond being of a type
usually assigned to infantry reconnaissance units,
several of which he knew to be operating as rear
security behind the main line when the atomic
exchange took place. The code words for "desperate situation" and "enemy armor" had also come
through, as well as portions of an in-the-clear
report indicating that the armor was of unknown
type and that many of his comrades had been tak-
en prisoner. Yeshev did not know, however, how
many pieces of armor, how many prisoners, or of
what rank. Neither did he know where all this was

taking place. Assuming that the message had been sent over field radio, he had to conclude that the action had occurred no more than fifty kilometers from this damnable, undependable bridge. That meant that the Americans—if it were the raider party, as he strongly suspected—could be even closer to Grabbe than he and with none of the obstacles that he was facing in between.

Yeshev sat back in his commander's chair and tried to will the knots of tension out of his back, while silently cursing the overrated German reputation for engineering efficiency.

He took a deep breath to clear his head of this pointless kvetching and decided what he had to do. The 2S9s that were already across the ravine would have to proceed alone toward Grabbe and try to intercept the American column alone, if it made a move on the village. They were crack crews in the 2S9s, each with kills notched against French and American tanks and APCs. But deep in his heart he doubted that they were any match for Americans who had trained in the commando tank tactics of Ross Kettle—damn his aboriginal eyes.

6

It was mid-afternoon before Tag was satisfied with the dispositions of his troops and vehicles. He laid a Bradley at each end of town, one on the slope above the grain silo by the tracks and the other on the grounds of an abandoned 18th-century monastery that overlooked the valley to the south. The No Slack Too he situated in the cavernous repair bays of a heavy-equipment shop on the north–south highway through town, giving himself a quick-response capability to support either of the APCs. He set full-complement watches in each of the Bradleys, but on three-hour rotations, and let the rest of the Rangers dismount and take up the quarters Goethe had offered in a farm workers' dormitory near the rail terminal and an empty guest house attached to the monastery. He ordered radio silence, except in case of enemy activity, and made certain that the Bradleys were thoroughly camouflaged, then took Prentice and went to the town jail, where Krager and a language teacher from the local gymnasium had been interrogating the prisoners.

The architecture of the building that housed the jail was appropriately mismatched among the Reformation facades and baroque statuary of the square. Its smooth-dressed stone and square pilasters topped by hard geometric capitals were clearly in the tradition of German public buildings of the 1930s, a collision of National Socialism and Art Deco, and the bare, hard-edged interior spaces only reinforced the aura of Teutonic discipline and efficiency. A graying watch captain met Tag and Prentice in the office foyer and led them down a back staircase to the cells and interrogation rooms in the basement.

Tag found Krager sitting with a small, bespectacled man in a large room that contained only three folding chairs and a metal desk. They were sitting in two of the chairs, Krager with his feet on the desk, drinking beer from bottles, laughing, and speaking in a language that seemed to be made up entirely of muttered stops and high-pitched vowels.

"Max, lieutenant," Krager said, waving them in the door with his beer bottle, "come on in and have a beer and meet Herr Klien. The sumbitch speaks Swahili. You fuckin' believe that?" He swung his heels off the desk and slapped the smaller man on the shoulder. Herr Klien grinned sheepishly and took a drink of beer and stood to take Tag's offered hand.

Tag introduced himself and Prentice, then sat on the edge of the desk and let Prentice take the empty chair.

"Gaylord," Tag said, "you are a goddamn wonder. Where the hell did you learn Swahili?"

"Oh, doing a little military-assistance work in East Africa a few years back. It was real handy among all those freakin' dialects. Couldn't cut a deal without it." Krager grinned and took a notebook out of the cargo pocket of his jumpsuit. "But I've got a few things here translated from the original Russian that I think you'd rather hear right now. You want a beer?" He leaned forward and pulled open a drawer of the desk full of bottles.

"Sure would," Tag said, passing a beer to Prentice. "How'd it go?"

"Well," Krager said, tipping back in his chair and nodding toward Herr Klien, "the professor here is a gem. Can you believe it? I was the good cop in the deal."

Tag arched his brows and glanced at Klien, who looked him squarely in the face, his pale, piercing eyes belying his diffident manner and soft speech.

"I reckon so," Tag said. "I only wish I'd been here to see it."

"Sumbitch is a tiger," Krager said. He took a long pull on his bottle and flipped open the notebook with his other hand. "You want it all, or you want me to cut to the chase?"

"We're here for the night," Tag said. "Let's work the long form."

Using the notebook more for a prop than for reference, Krager detailed the salient facts about the eleven men they had captured. They were all that remained of an infantry reconnaissance platoon that had been assigned to root out any Jagd Kommando or partisan units still operating behind the Soviet lines. Two squads of the platoon had been on a long-range patrol when the Allies' nuclear counter strike hit and had not been heard from since. The rest had survived by blind luck, just being in the right place at the right time. An underground silo had given them enough shelter to escape the worst effects of fallout and the radioactive rain, and their recently issued DKP-60 dosimeters had let them sniff their way around the worst areas of contamination, which is what they had been doing for more than three days, when they at last reached the town and tried to steal civilian vehicles, in the hope of making contact with an armored antitank contingent whose radio transmissions they had occasionally caught.

"So," Tag said to Krager, "what's your read on all this, Gaylord?"

Krager shrugged as he drained his bottle. He pulled another from the desk drawer, pried loose the cap on the drawer handle, and said, "Not a lot that we didn't expect, Max. These guys are beat. Hell, they'd give us the keys to the Kremlin for a good meal and a week on the Black Sea. From everything I gathered, I'd say these guys are pretty typical of what Ivan has left along the old front. They're scattered, without effective communication or mobility, hungry, scared. They're desperate but not really dangerous."

"What about the armor they were looking for?" Prentice asked.

"Yeah, that," Krager said, flipping the pages of his notebook. "Well, again, it pretty much confirms our latest gee-two. We couldn't get any of 'em to roll all the way over, but we cross-talked 'em enough that I'm satisfied the unit they had been monitoring is the same one in Grabbe, and that it's what's left of the escort for the nukes that you guys snuffed."

"Did you get any idea when their last contact was with the armor?" Tag asked.

"Hasn't really been any contact, Max," Krager replied. "Apparently, they've only been able to monitor. At least they say they haven't had any response or even acknowledgments of their own transmissions. Herr Klien and I are both inclined to believe 'em."

"Good enough," Tag said. "Anything else get stirred up in the prop wash?"

"Oh, some flotsam and jetsam, odds and ends. Seems like the morale was shot to hell, anyway, and the nukes caught our boys here by surprise. The way they figure it, they were left for dead before the first warhead was out of the tube, and I expect we'll find a lot of that running around." Krager riffed a few more pages of his notes, then went on. "I looked over their gear, but I didn't see anything new there; maybe the boys in gee-two can make something out of it, though. Besides that, there's nothing worth writing home about."

"No officers in the group?" Tag asked.

Krager shook his head. "A sergeant and a bunch of green kids."

"Okay," said Tag. He looked over to Prentice. "Chuck, get with Mayor Goethe again and see what he has for fuel, maybe do a little light scrounging, then go inspect our positions, and don't let those shitbirds of mine give you any guff. Gaylord and I are going to take a stroll and see if we can pick up anything from the citizenry." Turning to Klien, he said, "I hope you can help us out the rest of the afternoon, Herr Klien. There may be some folks here who know more than they realize."

"It would be my pleasure, Captain," Herr Klien replied.

The autumn sun slanted across the municipal square of Badenthaler, suffusing the air with a light like pollen, palpable as that cast in a painting by Vermeer. Tag and Krager walked out of the police building with Herr Klien and into this light that threw the ornate faces of the buildings across the square into shadowed relief. In the center of the square was a statuary group resembling the Laocoön but, if anything, more convulsed, and around the periphery the original street cobbles remained as a pedestrian walk. Along the side streets that radiated from the square, two- and three-story buildings of rusticated stone with beetling upper windows stood hip by flank, their ground floors containing shops and cafés and their upper floors offices and apartments. Behind them, neat gardens lined the alleys where residents met to talk on summer afternoons. But now the shops and cafés were closed for rationing, and there was no point in keeping an office open, lending the streets a Sunday silence that neither Tag nor Krager nor Herr Klien chose to break until they had walked several blocks.

At a modest neo-Gothic church at an intersection, Herr Klien stopped them and said, "Father Risser, the priest here, said he was hoping the monks from the new monastery on the mountain might come into town. They miss nothing, those fellows. So little in their lives, everything is an event."

"Sounds like you've been there," Tag said.

"I was born there, Captain," Herr Klien said, almost betraying a smile.

Tag blurted, "Born in a monastery," and Krager said at the same time, "But you're a Jew, Herr Klien."

Herr Klien cocked his head and raised his hand as though to a lecture hall full of rowdy boys. "During the Nazi war," he said, "those monks hid my mother and father and eventually me for more than six years in the old monastery, where your other small tank is parked. I learned my first alphabet from a monk—in Latin. I could read

Latin, Greek, Hebrew, and German all before I began my formal education, gentlemen. So, if I make sport of their life of withdrawal, I do it with great love and gratitude. Shall we go in?"

The rose windows of the church spread the afternoon light throughout its nave in a pastel spectrum that swept across the altar at the foot of a simple wooden crucifix. Herr Klien led them down the aisle and around the ambulatory behind the apse to a small office opposite a spartan chapel. Herr Klien knocked on the office door, and in a moment it was opened by a middle-age priest, who embraced Herr Klien and called him Rabi. The two men spoke a moment in German before Herr Klien turned to introduce Tag and Krager.

"Father Risser does not speak English," Herr Klien said as the priest shook hands with the two soldiers, "but he says he is very happy to know that people can still get in and out of here."

"Well," said Tag, "so are we. What about the monks?"

Herr Klien spoke with Father Risser and turned back to Tag.

"He says that only two boys have come down, two Swiss novices, who arrived last night. They are in the rectory next door, and we are welcome to speak to them."

Tag thanked the priest, and the three men went back out through the soft kaleidoscope of the nave.

It was past 1700 hours when Tag was through talking to the two novices and back at Mayor Goethe's office. The boys were young and frightened, but those contemplative eyes, as Herr Klien had predicted, did not miss much. On the eve of the nuclear exchange, seven or eight armored vehicles had crossed the mountain, heading not in the direction of Grabbe, however, but on a track farther north and west. Projecting how fast the slowest BMP could cover the terrain, Tag calculated that the Soviet unit could have made it to the green corridor running into Grabbe from the north before the exchange took place.

"So," he said to Prentice and Krager, pouring himself another cup of the mayor's coffee, "we're probably looking at three or four 2S9s and three or four BMPs. If they made it to Grabbe, they have fuel and rations, but their magazines have got to be about empty. Now, we can take these guys, but let's take 'em alive, if we can. Okay? They're lost and lonely, and if we can surprise them, we could bag the whole pack. Gaylord, that means you will have to find some way to keep a rein on N. Sain. He has a kind of weird discipline, and I seem to be able to push the right buttons on him, but I'll be damned if I can tell you how. Think you can handle it?"

Deep in a carved armchair, Krager grinned back at Tag. "When the Blade of Retribution meets the Child of Armageddon," he said, droning like a Tantric priest, "the Cosmic Coupling is complete, and dark entropy will find grace in the stillness."

"Yeah," Tag said, "I think you got it." Then, hearing footsteps in the hall, he looked toward the door and saw Fruits Tutti enter with a roll of printouts in his hand.

"Sorry to interrupt, Captain Max," Tutti said, "but I thought you'd wanna see dese."

"Whadda you got, Fruits?" Tag asked, rising from his perch on the edge of the desk.

"We got our Sundowner shots from de LandSat.

De angle's pretty flat, but de Beast did a good jobba cleanin' them up."

Fruits spread the rolled sheets on the leather blotter of the desk, overlapping their edges to form a single image of a large area of southern Germany.

"Now, Grabbe don't tell us shit, Captain Max," Fruits said, "but lookit dis." He pointed to where a blue-green tendril snaking into Grabbe from the west crossed a small river gorge. On one side of the gorge were a half-dozen pieces of small armor, and on the other side a column of about three times that many, including at least a dozen main battle tanks. From the flat angle of the satellite photo, the Beast, Fruits's computer program, had not been able to interpret the bridge across the river, and it appeared as only a smudge.

Prentice and Krager had joined Tag at the desk, and he turned to them now and said, "These guys *ain't* lost."

"Do you suppose," Prentice mused, "that some of those are the same ones we thought were in Grabbe?"

Without speaking or looking anyone in the eye, Krager took a pair of reading glasses out of his pocket, hung them on the end of his nose, bent over the satellite maps for a moment, then stood and quickly replaced the glasses in their case.

"Not our boys," he announced. "Whatever these six are on the eastern bank—and I think they're 2S9s—they're all the same type."

"What I want to know," Tag said, "is whether they're coming or going, whether they're all part of the same unit or just a bunch of strays. Any guesses?"

Prentice said, "Well, it looks to me like they are headed for Grabbe."

"Dat's what we thought, too, Lieutenant," Fruits said. "Dere'd be long shadows from de guns if dey was pointing the other way. So"—he looked to Tag—"whadda ya think, Captain Max?"

"I'm not sure, Fruits. I think you and Chuck are both right, that these guys are coming our way, but there's something not right. See the way the silhouettes are staggered here on the west bank? Those vehicles are not in formation to move, and these other six are definitely in a defensive posture. It may be that the bridge is as far as they're going, that they're just there to hold it and stop any of us from leaking through that seam out of Grabbe. What do you think, Gaylord?"

Krager shook his head. "I don't think Ivan would commit that much armor just to hold that one bridge," he said. "But I think you're right about their not being on the move, at least not when this picture was shot."

"Yeah," Tag said. "We're guessing, all right. Damn. And I'll bet Ivan knows that the radar and infrared on the night birds can't get through all the radiation, especially not with those hot spots on either side. All I see for it, gentlemen," he said, stepping away from the desk, "is to wait for the early-bird shots and see if there's been any overnight movement."

At that moment, there was another sound at the door, and the four soldiers all turned to meet Mayor Goethe. Herr Goethe, the model of civic dignity, had changed out of his soiled business suit and into an old, expensive tweed jacket and a pair of worsted trousers, and he was followed by a small, pretty young woman wearing a blue dress and carrying an open writing tablet across one forearm, her pen poised at the ready.

Herr Goethe stopped short of the desk, bowed slightly from the waist, and said, "Captain, our heating-oil truck has fuel for your tanks, but I need one of your men also to go to lead. Then we can have our beer and talk and later our beer and food and then, perhaps, some music—*ja!*"

Tag returned the bow. "Herr Mayor," he said, "we thank you, all of us, and we thank God that for one night we can put this war aside. Sergeant Tutti here can go with the truck."

Goethe introduced his assistant as Fräulein Di-Biassi, a Swiss–Italian who spoke German, Italian, and English and who would arrange for whatever Tag's men needed. She would show Fruits to the truck.

Tag thought that Fruits looked six inches taller as he left the office with the pretty girl with chestnut hair, speaking to her in a fractured Italian that made her laugh.

Tag sent Prentice and Krager back to their Bradleys, while he went to the No Slack Too to freshen up and set the watch rotation. Wheels and Ham were sitting on the rear deck of the tank playing cribbage when Tag got to the garage.

"There's our captain-about-town," Ham said. "Fruits find you with those pictures?"

"Yeah," Tag said, "we all had a look at them, and the bottom line is you slackassed suckers have a night off."

"No shit?" Wheels said, pushing up off his elbow. "And here I forgot my civvies."

"Wheelman," Ham said, "you know the Army ain't gonna let you have that much fun. What is the drill, Captain?"

"The mayor is laying a spread for us."

"With dancing girls, I guess," said Ham.

"Right," Tag replied. "In lederhosen."

"Shoot," Wheels said, "I don't care what kinda socks they's wearing. Is it, no shit, mixed company, Cap'n?"

"Whoa," said Tag. "You both sound like you been in the field too long."

"Well," Ham said, clearing his throat, "some of us have not had the, ahem, physical emoluments of others."

"At ease," Tag said. "You are free to make friends, but we'll have to rotate a watch. I want two of us here after dark, so if y'all want to go now and get a beer while I wash up, it's in the park on the square. But one of you get back here in thirty minutes, unless Tutti shows up, and in that case, I'll meet you there."

"Color us gone," Wheels said, and he and Ham were out the door.

Feeling almost guilty, somehow remiss in his duty, Tag nevertheless washed at a hand sink in a corner of the garage and changed into clean clothes from the skin out. He was running his electric razor over his chin a second time when Fruits Tutti arrived on the fuel-oil truck, jumping from the running board as it slowed and turning to wave and call in Italian to Fräulein DiBiassi, who sat in the cab and returned the wave.

"Uh, say, Captain Max," Fruits mumbled, still looking out the open door he had just backed through, "could I, uh, use ya razor when you're done?"

Tag glanced sideways at him. "Sure, Fruits," he said and shut up.

The scene on the square was so festive that it for a moment filled Tag with apprehension, as though in a world gone so wrong there was a thing that did not want this happiness to exist, and only he knew it. But just as quickly the feeling was gone, replaced by a soaring affection for the bravery of these people and their determination not to be denied life. He elbowed his way into the crowd and found Ham and Wheels hovering around a circle of beer kegs and the girls tapping them. Tag nodded to them, got a plastic cup of beer, and circulated through the throng, stopping briefly to talk with the mayor and Herr Klien, before circling back to the kegs to speak to his two men.

"Listen," he said to them, "if you two have any hope of heaven, you'll take the first night watch together."

"Well, I'm a Baptist, so I got no doubt," Wheels said, "but why's that, anyway?"

"You breathe a word of this to Tutti," Tag said, "and I'll personally remove your pancreas with a spoon, either of you, but the fact is that Mister Tutti has a sweety."

"Oh, fuck you and me both," Ham said. "*Our* Tutti Fruity?"

"I'll give you the full skinny later, just do it. Will you?"

"Oh, hell yes, Cap'n," Wheels said. "Won't there be a star waitin' in my crown when I get to heaven! Hot damn. If that boy gets laid, anything is possible, and all because of me."

"All right, then," Tag said, "drink up and get on back and relieve him. The mayor has opened up a beer hall for tonight just next to his office building. Tell Fruits to come on over there."

When Wheels and Ham had gone, Tag rejoined the mayor, and they walked together to the hall.

With all its tables set, the hall would hold perhaps four hundred, Tag estimated, but fewer than half that many were laid for tonight, and one end of the hall had been cleared for a low stage, upon which sat amplifiers, microphones, a drum set, an electronic keyboard, and a variety of other instruments, from saxophones to electric guitars. Already the Rangers as well as the citizens of Badenthaler were into the spirit of the evening, offering frothy toasts and laughing at everything as waitresses sailed out of the kitchen bearing huge trays of food.

Herr Goethe led Tag to a half-full table for twelve and introduced him to his wife and two other city officials and their wives—and, of course, Fräulein DiBiassi, whom he knew—then they all sat and watched the food arrive, and it was definitely not standard beer-hall fare.

Every table was set with platters of tiny wursts and pickles, all right, but also with pâtés, pots of butter, green salad bright with radish slices and wedges of tomato, great tureens of pale corn-broth soup, bowls of spaetzle dumplings, and a mountain of bread rolls, in addition to endless steins of wonderful local beer. Carvers pushed steam carts through the hall, slicing custom slabs of roasts, hams, sauerbratens, and geese, while other carts dispensed potatoes, kraut, fresh peas, spinach-and-egg casserole, and carrots piqued with dill. Fruits Tutti joined Tag's table somewhere between the beef and peas and sat next to Fräulein DiBiassi without being asked. *Miracles of miracles,* Tag thought, *he found a uniform that fits.*

By the time the cakes and strudels and coffee arrived and a band of teenagers was tuning up on stage, Tag noticed that Mad Dog and Rabies had arrived to join N. Sain at a far table. All three were, more or less, in uniform, but their hair and car-

riage gave the lie to any military impersonation,
and the civic leaders of Badenthaler couldn't keep
their eyes off the trio any more than Tag could,
especially when he saw MD and Rabies lean in
toward N. Sain and all of them look toward the
stage.

Tag had an impulse to say something to Herr
Goethe, but he let the good feeling of food and
beer soak in and thought, *Oh, what the hell.
Let it roll.* He saw Rabies rise from the table
across the hall. Tall, stooped, and almost pre-
ternaturally pale, the musician-soldier shuffled
across the open floor to the stage like a B-movie
zombie, spoke—actually spoke—something to
one of the boys there, then turned and motioned
MD and N. Sain to come over. MD slid behind
the trap set, pumped the bass to get its feel,
rapped out a few lightning riffs on the snares
and tom-toms, and adjusted the height of the
cymbals, while Rabies tried the stops on the keyboard and N. Sain lashed himself to an electric
guitar. One of the boys from the band held on
to his electric bass, grinning nervously at another who stood fingering a tenor sax and licking
its reed.

N. Sain cut a lick down the neck of the guitar,
drew down the last note, and settled into an
intricate walking blues, followed by the drums,
the keyboard, and the bass player. Following N.
Sain's lead, the music built in tempo and complex-
ity, until the sixteen-bar variations bent beyond
the pale of rock and shattered against a crescendo
of rim shots and cymbals. The place went wild,
and, Tag had a hunch, these maniacs were just
warming up.

A familiar piano lead brought them into "Good

Golly, Miss Molly," and Rabies opened his mouth to the microphone on the stand in front of him and filled the speakers with a wild, driving, note-for-note imitation of the Killer, Jerry Lee Lewis, the first words Tag had ever heard from Rabies.

Two adolescent girls hit the floor to dance, followed by a boy and a girl, and then there was Krager. He was leading a reluctant woman, but even at a distance Tag could tell that her protests were useless. Krager loved looking like the very opposite of a dancer, and Tag suspected it was because Gaylord knew that he was good. He spun his partner into a dip, rolled her out in a double spin, and they were instantly in full jitterbug. Whoever Krager had picked on turned out to be a fine dancer, and Herr Goethe confirmed that she was a gymnastics teacher. Applause rattled the beams, and even N. Sain popped his fingers twice in front of the microphone when they were done. Tag turned to say something to Tutti and found that he was gone—he and Fräulein DiBiassi.

N. Sain and his sidemen played a short set, then turned the instruments over to the local boys and walked back to their table like victorious television wrestlers leaving the ring. Tag stayed long enough to be convinced that Fruits wasn't coming back, excused himself, and walked through the deserted streets to the garage where the No Slack Too was parked.

"Any sign of Tutti?" Tag asked Ham Jefferson as he entered the bay.

"Not a shadow," Ham said. "You want one of us to stick around until he gets back?"

"Naw," Tag said. "He'll show. I can keep a lid on it till he gets here. They're holding your reservations at the beer hall, so take off."

Minutes after Ham and Wheels had gone, Tag heard something outside the ajar door to the garage and walked toward it through the shadows along the wall, stopping when he could see through the crack into the moonlit street outside. Fräulein DiBiassi stood astraddle of her bicycle, letting it slip sideways as she held Fruits with both arms and kissed him on the mouth. Fruits, for his part, held her waist as though it were an egg. She pulled her head back, laughed, and said something into his ear. Fruits wrapped his arms around her and held her close. Tag could see his loader's shoulders shaking with emotion. Feeling embarrassed, Tag withdrew from the door and slipped noiselessly back to the No Slack Too.

When Fruits at last came inside, he was wearing a flushed, loopy grin and had lost his fatigue cap. One leg of his jumpsuit was unbloused, and there was a smear of lipstick on his smooth-shaven cheek.

"Hey," he said a little too loudly, too obviously trying to steer anything Tag had to say away from himself, "I'm not late or anything, am I? Ham and Wheels already gone?"

Tag was sitting on the lip of the commander's hatch. He put down the logbook he was pretending to read and said, "You're right on the money, Fruits. I cut the guys loose a little early." He dropped the log between his knees into the seat below, swung his feet out of the hatch, and slid down the glacis. "You decide not to stick around for all of N. Sain's set?"

Fruits blushed to his ears. "Uh, huh-uh, naw," he stammered. "Luisa, she don't like dat music much—that's Fräulein DiBiassi, I mean. She set up all the computers in the city offices—didja know that, Captain?"

"So naturally you wanted to see them. Right?"

"Well, yeah, sure," Fruits said. "Never know whatcha might learn."

"Well," Tag said, stretching, "she's a pretty girl and you are a pearl without price, Francisco. I hope you two made real good friends."

Fruits blushed to his scalp. "Yeah," he said. "Yeah. I didn't know, I mean, you know, I ain't never . . ."

"Yeah," said Tag, grinning back at Fruits, "I do know. Now, you sit up and think about it, and I'm going to grab some rack."

Fruits didn't wake Tag for the last watch until the early-bird satellite photos came in at 0615. What Tag saw on them did nothing to improve his morning.

The six 2S9s were gone and, as Tag could tell from the early-bird's higher angle, so was the bridge in the narrow corridor leading into Grabbe from the west. The rest of the column was still stuck on the other side of the river gorge, but they appeared to be reorganizing to move, as well. Wherever the 2S9s had gone, they were well concealed when these pictures were shot fifteen minutes earlier and could easily be in Grabbe already.

"Fruits," Tag said, "run these back through the Beast and get me the radiation overlays on them." And while Fruits was printing out the new maps, Tag roused Ham and Wheels and radioed the Bradleys to be ready to move ASAP in full NBC gear. He looked at the sheets that came off the laser printer, cocked his head in concentration, and called his crew in from readying the XM-F4.

"Okay, sweethearts, here's the dip: Grabbe is being reinforced, but I think we still have a chance to get the jump on them. As the crow flies, it's less than twenty kilometers to Grabbe, over pretty good country. But to do that, we're going to have to split the seam between two very warm pockets. If Barlow wasn't bullshitting us about what the Bradleys can do, it shouldn't be any problem. But if it does get too hot for them, I'm taking us in anyway. Anybody think better?"

"Oh, Bossman," Ham said, "I always wanted to be squeezed in between two high yellows."

"Oh, yeah," Wheels said sarcastically, "it's a real dream come true. Let's get it."

At 0650, Tag led his column out of Badenthaler, disappearing over the ridge above the valley to the southwest and into the area of highest radioactivity that they had yet faced, a mere slit where the tactical radii of two neutron detonations had failed to overlap, but it would save them more than fifteen kilometers and put them in Grabbe in less than an hour.

The No Slack Too quartered across a repetition of low ridges, through fields and vineyards, breaking trail for the Bradleys. Tag had to halt them beyond each crest to double-check the radiation count ahead, and as he did he scanned the countryside on either flank, surveying the effects of the neutron warheads. Explosive force, Tag knew, counted for little of the 'tron's effects: it was designed to kill with massive waves of radiation, leaving vehicles and structures intact. Less than three kilometers from the detonation point of each 'tron, and with his commander's scope at full magnification, Tag could attest those effects all too well.

The late fruits, apples and pears, hung blackened in drooping, leafless orchards, and the grasses of the meadows were discolored, curled, and lifeless as ash. Twice already Tag had again seen sick, irradiated cattle staggering through fields of carcasses, but nothing was more pitiful than the image of the sheep, the boys, and their dogs that leapt into his scope when he halted beyond the fourth ridge.

Panning to his left, Tag followed the crest of the next approaching ridge to where it fell into the valley and spread in a weedy meadow. In the middle of the meadow lay a bunched flock of sheep, and to either side of them a dead dog. Behind the animals were the bodies of two boys, one still holding a long stick in his hand. It was as though they had simply dropped dead — sheep, dogs, and shepherds — without a clue to what had killed them. One moment they were peacefully gathering their flock in the cool predawn, and in the next their cells were exploding like microwaved eggs. Tag saw, for a searing instant, the deliverance N. Sain sought in death, and it angered him that these deaths were not more gruesome, that they gave an illusion of bloodless necessity to the terrible truth of war, its horror, and its madness. It angered him too that, although these deaths were not the last, it would be a century before men could live again on this rich and lovely highland.

Tag swept his radiation counter in an arc before them and said to Wheels, "Looks like we're out of the pinch, Wheelman. Hold your bearing, and let's goose it up a little."

Wheels responded with quarter throttle, and the No Slack Too gathered speed down the grade and held it up the next rise, the two Bradleys keep ing pace in close formation behind. From the top of the next ridge, Tag saw what he expected: a road cutting through a tree farm, the last leg of their fast route into Grabbe before taking again to the main road from Badenthaler.

"Spread your interval," Tag radioed to the Bradleys, and the APCs dropped back, veering to either side to break the axis of the column, and it was none too soon. As Tag directed Wheels onto the rock road, about three-hundred meters from where it entered the row-cropped timber, a tube-fired Songster missile whooshed from the 120mm multi-gun on a 2S9 inside the trees and crashed into the turret of the XM-F4, puddling a shallow depression in the slick-skin armor and jolting the men inside in their seats.

Even thrown sideways in his gunner's chair, Ham could see the heat signature of the missile launch on his target-acquisition scope and instinctively called out, "Target."

"Confirmed," Tag responded as he coordinated his scope with Ham's and took the Phalanx controls. "Shoot."

Tag touched off the first burst from the Phalanx milliseconds before Ham released the HE round from the main tube. The combination of 120mm high explosives and the uranium slugs from the Phalanx tore open the nose of the compact Soviet tank, spilling smoke and fire like a gush of blood. At the same moment, a second 2S9 in the trees on the other side of the road loosed its Songster, which struck the No Slack Too full in the side, caromed off the slick slope of the fender, and exploded in an angry, black crab above the tank's rear deck, scouring it with shrapnel.

Before Tag and his crew could respond, an ATGM

sprang from the rack on top of N. Sain's Bradley and obliterated the Soviet position, leaving only three smoking trunks in the gaping hole that had been a line of firs. What remained of the 2S9 was missing its turret and most of the turret deck. Its burning commander sat headless in his seat.

"Stack up," Tag commanded over the TacNet, ordering the Bradleys back into column. "Follow me."

"Wheels," he said to the driver, "hit the road and give it all that the Bradleys can stand. Something tells me that Ivan isn't as demoralized as we thought."

"And," Ham Jefferson added, "so much for our sneaky-poo element of surprise."

The road was good, flat, and slightly downhill, and the loaded Bradleys had no trouble keeping up the ninety kilometers per hour pace that Wheels set as the regular rows of evergreens flashed past on either side, with Tag half expecting another ambush behind each one. They crossed the tree farm in ten minutes and without incident, however, until they came to the highway that linked Grabbe with Badenthaler.

The No Slack Too skidded off the rock road onto the pavement and into a storm of 73mm cannon fire and the intersecting contrails of rockets.

"Ambush!" Tag shouted through the intercom and the TacNet simultaneously, and the crew of the XM-F4 leapt into action. Ham locked on the first blip on his screen and loosed a 120mm HE round into a Soviet BMP's position in the edge of the trees, while Tag took control of the Phalanx and scoured the other side of the highway with a jet of uranium slugs that perforated a second BMP like a colander. The third Soviet APC laid in the ambush exploded in its rear and lurched forward onto the shoulder of the road boiling smoke, followed shortly by N. Sain's careening Bradley, which shot straight across and into the blighted orchard on the other side just as three more 2S9s came tearing up the road in echelon formation. Two rockets from the lead tank smashed into the upper glacis of the No Slack Too, driving it backward on its tracks and stalling the turbines.

In the moment while the screens and computer systems blinked to restore themselves, Tag ordered Ham to shoot on manual, and the round struck the first 2S9 where its tread met the road, spinning the toy tank ninety degrees and ripping off its drive carriage on one side. It settled in the middle of the road, immobilized but still fighting, its turret snapping around for another shot at the No Slack Too as the multi-gun on a second 2S9 roared.

Wheels had the turbines restarted before the crippled Soviet tank could bring its gun to bear. Prentice's Bradley, tearing across the highway during the exchange, took the shot from the second 2S9 high on its heavy forward slick-skin armor. Sergeant White, Prentice's driver, was slapped unconscious by the concussion, and Rangers were scattered all through the troop compartment, but the armor, though contorted by the blast, was not breached, and Prentice took the controls and kept them going.

"Butcher Boy," he radioed to Tag, "this is Lazarus. We're hit. We're still up but have taken a hit."

Playing his final option, Tag barked out coordinates and ordered the Bradleys due south, through the dark yellow apron of the neutron zone they had been skirting, toward a speck of green deep within the swath of nuclear devastation. And even as he did, a HE round from one of the two charging 2S9s pummeled the No Slack Too's turret, causing an automatic cyclone response from the Gatling barreled Phalanx, which Tag had programmed to return any incoming fire. But before Tag could confirm any hits, Wheels had thrown the tank into a bootlegger's turn and accelerated to the south after the speeding Bradleys.

7

Within two kilometers down the continuation of the rock road to the south, the No Slack Too had overtaken the Bradleys, and as the radiation count rose steadily beyond levels the Soviets could tolerate, Tag slowed his column and called for situation reports. His own systems checked out OK, despite the fusillade of direct hits that the XM-F4 had absorbed, and N. Sain's APC was unscathed. Prentice, however, had lost a vision port and one rack of ATGMs, and the protective boot over his Phalanx's gun mantle was perforated. Nothing could leak inside the Bradley from the Phalanx cupola, but it meant that the innards could be hot and dirty, and no one could work on the gun in the field if anything broke down.

Satisfied that they were still operational, Tag moved the column forward at a crawl, searching the territory before them with his sensors for the path of least contamination which would eventually lead them to the oasis of green on his maps. The blighted landscape that they passed through was becoming familiar to Tag but no less repugnant. There were more civilian dead lying bloated in the open here where the initial radiation had been more intense, mostly people who had been out early to do farm chores, and whole herds of

131

dairy cattle had fallen dead in their tracks, stippling the fields with mottled, lifeless patches of black and white, the swollen carcasses looking like the inflated figures from a cartoon, although Tag saw no humor in the comparison.

The column's progress was agonizingly slow, and Tag filled part of the morning updating the logbook and encoding a series of transmissions he hoped to relay from the nuclear-free pocket they were approaching. The ferocity of the ambush had taken him by surprise, but one part of his mind was still curious about why there had not been more firepower turned on them. There were only two possible approaches to Grabbe from the north and the east, and he estimated there were at least a dozen pieces of armor already in the village before the 2S9s arrived, yet by his count there had been only the 2S9s and three BMPs involved. He needed to get to Grabbe and find out the conditions behind this; there might be some important G-2 in all that. His other nagging concern was for the men in the Bradleys. The NBC defenses were holding up well, but they were already spending more time in hot areas than he had calculated for the entire mission, and if the Rangers were forced out of the APCs, their suits and masks would be at best marginal protection in any of the country between here and home. They left the road crossed a rain-swollen brook, climbed the ridge beyond it, and the radiation count began to drop. It was just past 1200 hours.

The place they were going was an anomaly for more than being radiation free. The small village sat on a bench of high ground far from any watercourse or railroad, but it was the site of a variety of mineral springs and had enjoyed a

minor reputation as a spa among budget-minded
vacationers. From the details of its layout that
Tag called up from his computer atlas, he could
see that the narrow streets meandered among a
quaint collection of old stone buildings and siz-
able wooden homes set on narrow lots, many
of them, he suspected, doubling as pensions or
small hotels. Near the center of town, where
many of the twisting streets converged, there was
a congregation of buildings that he took to be
the bathhouses and recreation arcades of the spa
proper. At the outskirts of the town, after traveling the last two kilometers through essentially
clean territory, Tag halted his column at an abandoned château and ordered the vehicles swept for
radiation while the men stretched their legs and
chowed down.

He was relieved to discover that there was a
minimum of contamination clinging to his armor,
and even the Phalanx on Prentice's Bradley was
not yet too hot to handle, at least in an NBC suit,
so he ordered the men to patch the synthetic boot
on its mantle and then change into fresh protective gear. While Ham and Wheels were hosing
down all three vehicles with absorbent foam and
spray from the No Slack Too's pressure washer,
Tag gave Fruits the messages he wanted burped
up to the communications satellite, then took
Prentice and Krager with him upstairs in the
château for another look at the village before
they went in.

Sitting in an attic dormer, Tag swept the village with his binoculars before passing them to
Prentice.

"Chuck," he said, "look over there just to the
right of the bathhouse complex and tell me what

you see. I think my eyes are playing tricks."

Prentice looked at Tag quizzically, held the glasses to his eyes, adjusted the focus, and let his jaw drop open an inch.

"No," he said. "Huh-uh. Can't be."

"Here," Krager said, wedging himself into the small dormer between Tag and Prentice, "let one of us enlisted swine have a peek."

"Okay," Prentice said, handing him the glasses, "but I'm telling you, it's some weird shit, sergeant."

Krager twisted the focus and found the place Tag had indicated. Sitting nose to nose in the broad promenade around the bathhouses were two Soviet T-64B tanks, their muzzles elevated and something sticking out of each one.

"That's fucking *flowers*," Krager said.

"Thank you, Gaylord," Tag said, "for the candor of your rank. That's what I thought, but I wasn't going to be the first to say it. See any movement?"

Krager passed the glasses slowly over the town. "Huh-uh," he said. "Looks way too quiet to me."

Tag nodded. "I had been thinking we might just bypass the vil itself, but this needs to be checked out. Like you said, Chuck, this is some weird shit. I'll lead us in with the top down, but I want all weapons primed and your Bradleys to stay buttoned up. Once we're in those streets, there's not going to be much room to maneuver, so make sure you're looking a couple of moves ahead, so you'll have someplace to scat if things get hot. Let's get in, see what we can see, and get the hell out of there. We've still got fish to fry in Grabbe."

Back at the No Slack Too, Tag called up the street plan again on his VLD and plotted different routes through the village for each of the vehicles, allowing the Bradleys to filter in on streets roughly parallel to his own approach, while keeping all of them from being jammed up at the same time in any place too tight to fight from. He programmed the LandNav to take them back out on automatic if it came to a running fight, then took his place in the open turret and ordered Wheels to move out.

The small town was a picture of shabby gentility. Tag eased the No Slack Too between colorless stone buildings and the peeling facades of once-quaint wooden houses now wrapped in an aura of creeping desuetude. But for several twisting blocks, he saw no signs of life except a pair of cats that streaked between two alleys and stopped in the narrow noon shadow against a wall to glare at the passing tank. Tag touched the mini-gun mount beside him nervously.

Two blocks from the bathhouses, a second street joined the one Tag was traveling to form a broad avenue lined with sidewalk cafés and tourist shops with dusty windows. The Cinzano and Martini umbrellas on the café tables were all furled, and the shops were dark behind their dingy glass. Tag heard the sound of a starter grinding behind him, followed by a revving motor. "Movement to the rear," he called over the intercom, and he grabbed the mini-gun and spun it around. A long school bus pulled jerkily from a side street and lurched to a halt, blocking the avenue. Tag could see no one in it, not even in the driver's seat.

"Movement front," he heard Wheels say, and Tag whipped himself around to face forward, where another bus had appeared to seal the

other end of the block. It too seemed empty.

"Lazarus, Disciple," Tag radioed, "we're being
blocked in. Back out. Back out."

"Butcher Boy," Prentice responded, "this is Lazarus. No can do. We have dump trucks front and
rear, but no personnel."

"O Avatar of Ambush," N. Sain crooned over
the airwaves, "we too are idled in the cosmic current."

"All units," Tag commanded, "stand to, but
hold your fire." Then he shouted down through
the turret, "Wheels, put me on the bullhorn."

"Hello," Tag said over the external loudspeaker,
his amplified voice echoing in the still, empty street. "Hello. Come out. Show yourselves.
No one will be hurt." Sweat was running from
beneath his CVC and down the back of his neck
inside the NBC suit.

A girl of no more than twelve or thirteen, wearing a plaid jumper and yellow blouse, stepped from
a doorway down the street, followed by another,
then more from all the adjacent buildings, until
the No Slack Too was surrounded by three or four
dozen girls dressed all alike and each holding a
spray of flowers or a loaf of bread. Without a
word, they converged on the tank, holding the
bread and flowers in their outstretched hands,
smiling faintly.

Things had already proved strange inside the
killing zone, but the apparition of these young
faces was like petals on a dead bough, the strangest
Tag had yet seen. One of the girls tossed her bou-
quet to Tag, who caught it in both hands at the
same instant that he caught the movement on
the roofs out of the corner of his eye. He froze

and said softly through his CVC, "Uh-oh. We got people on the roofs. Be easy now."

Tag's calm belied the racing pinwheel of possibilities that spun and sparked across his consciousness. Was this some sort of mass hysteria? A common dementia from radiation poisoning? An insidious Soviet ploy, using children to screen an ambush? But no shots were fired, and he immediately got a grip on his thoughts. Still holding the flowers in both hands, he turned slowly and looked up to the roofs. Men with rifles and rocket-propelled grenades stood behind the stone cornices and wooden gingerbread of the upper facades, holding their weapons at port arms, menacing but not threatening, like good bouncers in a rough roadhouse. None of them was in a uniform.

Moving with slow deliberation, Tag lay the flowers on the top of the turret, eased off his CVC and put it under one arm, smoothed his hair, and said in the most casual voice he could muster, "Thanks for the flowers. Who's in charge here, fellas?"

In answer, the girls melted away from the front of the tank to make way for a man coming down the middle of the street. He was bareheaded and unshaven, and his Soviet uniform had been stripped of all insignia, but he walked with an easy military bearing, never taking his dark, hooded eyes off Tag.

"You are welcome to the flowers," the man said, coming to a stop among the girls. "Who are you? And why are you here?" His voice was even and unchallenging but with the stiffness of command.

"I am Captain Max Tag, United States Army," Tag said. "This tank and our two other vehicles are my command. We are here," he continued, not wanting to reveal anything this man didn't need to know, "because your comrades in Grabbe ambushed us, and we had no place else to run. And whom do I have the pleasure of addressing?"

"We need to talk, Captain," said the man. "Tell your men please to stand in the hatches, so we can see their hands, and you please to come down. I am Milos Popper, and I have no comrades in Grabbe."

Tag gave the order and climbed down from the turret. Milos Popper came forward and nodded without offering Tag a hand, then turned and walked to a sidewalk table outside a café, where Tag joined him, and one of the girls brought them two bottles of the local mineral water.

"So," Popper said conversationally, "did the war not end itself, or are you just mopping out the survivors?"

The sarcasm was not lost on Tag, but he would not rise to it. "I'm happy there are survivors," he said, raising his bottle to Popper. He took a long drink and continued. "There's a cease-fire on right now. Your side and my side . . ."

Popper raised a hand to stop him. "I have no side, Captain," he said, "but please to go on."

"*Both* sides," Tag said, "agreed to call things off after they saw what nuclear war really means. It's not an armistice or a truce, but it could lead to that if we can keep your . . . the Soviet forces from attempting something reckless here in the southern sector. Our job is to reconnoiter here within the nuclear strike zone, survey the effects, and make sure the First Guards do not attempt to break through. Like I said, we were headed to Grabbe when we were attacked and had to run here through a radiation area to get away. What brings you here?"

Popper sipped his mineral water and studied Tag for a full minute before he answered.

"I was part of the garrison at Grabbe," he said. "Three platoons of Russian tanks and BMPs and one of Czech, my own, were stationed there. We had been in reserve throughout the fighting, because the Russians did not trust us. But they had good reason. We Czechs have been very unwilling cooperators, Captain Tag, and the more we saw of the course of the war, and the more we talked among ourselves, the more convinced we became that we had no business, as you say, in this war. By good fortune, we deserted en masse on the eve of the nuclear exchange and were in hiding near here when the bombardment took place. We surrendered to the local mayor, disarmed our vehicles, and pledged ourselves to a separate peace. We can still defend ourselves, Captain, but we will not be part of this war."

"And what about us?" Tag asked.

"You may go, or you may stay," Popper told him. "But if you stay, you must disarm your vehicles and pledge yourselves to peace. If you leave, it must be at once."

As desirable as peace was, Tag did not hesitate to say, "Then we had best be going. We'll send someone for you."

"Captain," Popper said, "we have no desire to leave, not until this war is settled at least. Tell your superiors that. Finish your water; it is quite healthful."

"Is there anything we can do for you?" Tag asked. "We can get food or medical supplies dropped in."

"Captain, the last thing we need is to be attention. No, just leave. Forget we are here for now, that is the best thing you can do for us."

Tag drained his mineral water, thanked Popper, and went back to the No Slack Too. He contacted Prentice and N. Sain and told them what to do, then when the buses were backed out, he retraced his route into town and regrouped with the Bradleys at the empty château.

It had not been easy and it had cost him one T-80, but Yeshev had at last managed to get the rest of his column through the ravine and across the river, and now he was rolling smartly along a paved road, only a few kilometers from their destination. He had been gratified by the news he received from his advanced unit that, despite their own losses, his men had met and driven off the American armor. Less heartening was the cryptic situation report that held nearly half the regular garrison at Grabbe to be "intact/inoperable" with no mention of casualties. But it was the men in the dozen vehicles from his lost patrol he most wanted to see, and they had, in fact, made it to Grabbe.

The commander of his detachment of 2S9s met Yeshev at the edge of town, and the man's explanation of the situation inside Grabbe did nothing to brighten Yeshev's day. The men of the patrol were exhausted, hungry, and badly shaken by their experience on the nuclear battlefield, but they were still able and willing to fight and had contributed to the attack on the Americans. It was the remains of the regular garrison that posed the problem.

Yeshev learned that not only had the Czech platoon deserted but two of the remaining armored platoons had taken up positions on the high ground to the south of town, their guns trained on Grabbe, and refused to rejoin the unit or move from where they were.

"Goddamn it, man," Yeshev bellowed at the 2S9 commander, "they're soldiers. They cannot just quit. Did you order them to come in?"

"I ordered them, Comrade Colonel," the tanker said, "and they refused."

"But they made no threats, correct?"

"Yes, Comrade Colonel, that is correct."

Yeshev quit his fuming. "Very well," he said. "To hell with them—for now. Take me to the men from the convoy."

Tag was hung on the horns of a dilemma—or perhaps a "trilemma"— he thought, as he scowled at the images on the VLD before him. He was more determined than ever to reach Grabbe, so returning to the Jagd Kommando support base was out of the question, but neither of his approaches to Grabbe from here had much to recommend it. He could return the way they had come and be almost certain there would be armor waiting for him, or he could continue west before turning back north through unknown territory and try to enter Grabbe from the southwest. The entire route was long and peppered with radiation, but it looked better and better the more he studied the maps.

With that, he ordered his men to double-check all NBC gear and systems, made a quick survey of their fuel status, and produced printout maps of their proposed route for Prentice, Krager, and N. Sain. The column swept north and west around the peaceful spa and entered the margin of nuclear fallout scattered by an explosive blast.

Inside his zipped NBC suit, Tag swore he could feel the heat of radiation from the ravaged landscape around them. Slightly more than two kilometers from ground zero, they were close enough to see firsthand the physical devastation of atomic war. The expanding, hardening envelope of air that was driven outward from ground zero had sheared off tall trees and the upper stories of buildings and stripped the earth of every piece of loose debris, leaving stark ruins in a scoured plain. The intense heat that followed ignited all but stone and steel, and then the flames were sucked back toward the center by the air collapsing into the vacuum it had left behind. Those trees still standing—in places, whole orchards of them—were blackened skeletons. The flattened homes and farms could have been the work of centuries, not of seconds. And everywhere there were the deadly, irradiated rocks dropped from the nuclear cloud, like spores from mushroom gills.

Sacrificing speed for the safety of the men in the Bradleys, whose NBC systems Tag could not be as confident of as he was of those of the No Slack Too, the column tacked among the hot spots and the pox of irradiated rocks that turned the countryside into a moonscape. It was more than an hour before Tag could turn them back northeast, still hugging the perimeter of the dead zone, and begin their final approach on Grabbe.

Yeshev was less sanguine about his unit's performance against the Americans after he had talked to the survivors of the nuclear convoy and learned the details of the losses in the latest ambush outside Grabbe. Especially vexing to him was the report of one of the American APCs taking a direct hit from one of his 2S9s and not being stopped. He was familiar enough with Kettle's theories and with the field intelligence on the American tank to surmise a lot of what it could do—his own T-80B had been built with many of Kettle's ideas in mind—but that there were Bradleys able to survive in tandem with it was not something Yeshev had calculated. It was clearer than ever to him, however, that if he were to find a route out for the First Guards and save his career and his life, he had to eliminate the Americans.

Yeshev rearmed the survivors of the convoy with ammunition and missiles from his recon column, set outposts at the possible approaches to the town from the north, east, and west, then assembled his combined forces, now numbering twenty-eight pieces of mixed armor, in addition to the outposts, and moved them out of town in assault formation toward the emplacements of the renegade garrison in the hills south of town.

"Cap'n," Wheels Latta said as he brought them over a low rise, "tank formation dead ahead about a halfa klick."

"You sure, Wheels?" Tag asked. He had been looking left when they topped the high ground.

"I just had a glimpse, Cap'n," Wheels replied, "but I don't think I could miss that."

Tag halted his column just below the crest of the next rise. Now out of the fallout zone, he left the No Slack Too, climbed the rest of the way on foot, and lay in the grass on top, trying to focus his binoculars through the visor of the NBC suit. Finding that impossible, he unzipped the cowl of the suit, peeled it back, and settled again on his elbows. The glasses at once confirmed Wheels's sighting. About four-hundred meters in front of him, on the last high ridge before the land fell into the plain, Tag could see nine of the 2S9-type compact tanks and three BMPs in AT configuration, all dug into fighting positions and all with their weapons trained on Grabbe. Things, Tag concluded, were getting curiouser and curiouser.

Yeshev dispersed his formation into the cover of the last buildings on the south side of Grabbe, about twelve-hundred meters from the mutineers' positions, pulled his own T-80B into the open, and opened up a frequency to hail the men on the ridge. He had already determined that he would not fire on his own soldiers unless they fired first, but neither would he risk the main body of his force in an attempt to encircle and capture the garrison. His hope was that some combination of persuasion and bluff would turn the trick.

"Ferret," he said into his radio, using the garrison's open call sign, "this is Alpha Fox Actual. Did you receive my instruction to rejoin my element? Over."

"We received that instruction, Fox," a voice replied.

"Will you comply?"

"No," the voice said. "We will not."

"And have you considered the consequences?"

Yeshev heard a snort of derision before the voice said, "We prefer the consequences of living, Fox.

And if we are to die, it will be by our own choice, for our own reasons, in our own cause. We will not die for any more lies, any more Grand Gambits."

Yeshev let the air hang dead. There was a fervor, almost a hysteria in the voice on the radio. If this was any indication of the morale and attitudes among the scattered forces, the idea of the First Guards regrouping and fighting its way free was even more unlikely than it already seemed, and his odds of success were almost nil. In weighing the possible consequences for himself, throwing in his lot with the renegades was not without appeal. Yeshev recoiled from the temptation with strong words.

"Ferret," he said, "you have five minutes to abandon your positions and rejoin my element, or I will take measures to bring you down."

Back inside the No Slack Too, Tag said to his crew, "It looks to me like the rest of the garrison that our Czech buddy left behind has decided about what he did. There's about a dozen pieces of Ivan's armor dug in up there, with their guns laid on the town. So let's not go running up the six of the formation. Wheels, look on the map. See that knob off to our right? Keep us behind this ridge until we're just below it, then cut back for it. That will give us a flank position."

"That's a done deal, Cap'n," the driver said.

Tag radioed instructions to the Bradleys, and the three vehicles wheeled right and accelerated.

Yeshev knew he had talked himself into a corner, and so did every one of his commanders, but only he knew it was a bluff. He moved four tanks forward on each flank, and the turrets on the mutineers' tanks came to life, tracking the movement with their guns.

The knoll Tag had chosen for their position was only slightly lower than the line of renegade tanks and enough in advance of it to provide targets all along its length. That was what Tag had anticipated. But he was momentarily undone by the sight of Yeshev's battle group jockeying into position below. Although he had only a clue to the reasons, the situation was obvious, and if the shooting started, he wanted to be on someone's side. He held the Bradleys back and had Wheels move into a shallow dimple in the knoll, where only the turret of the No Slack Too had to be exposed for a shot in either direction.

Ham worked his fingers furiously, programming dozens of possible targets into his sights. "Hey, Boss," he said, "what's the drill? They got more tanks than we got bullets."

"This one's off the books, Ham. Load a sabot and stand by."

While the carousel spun a sabot round into the main tube, Tag keyed the full range of Soviet battle frequencies and announced over the air, "All hail. All hail. Soviet armor south of Grabbe, cease your advance. I say again, cease your advance."

The commanding voice shocked Yeshev like a douse of cold water, sending shivers down his back. Like every tanker, one of his secret fears was to be in the open under an enemy's guns and not know where that enemy is. At the same time a wave of relief flooded through him, for without yet knowing exactly how, he sensed that the unexpected appearance of the Americans might give him some face-saving way out of the stand-off. He halted his flankers and replied to Tag in English.

"Unknown source, this is Alpha Fox, identify yourself. Over."

"Alpha Fox, this is Butcher Boy, NATO cease-fire monitor. Be advised you are operating in a demilitarized zone in violation of international agreements, and your presence has been report-ed."

"Butcher Boy, we have no knowledge of cease-fire monitors. You be advised that this is an inter-nal situation. . . ."

"Butcher Boy, Butcher Boy." A third voice broke into the transmission. "This is Ferret, commander on the high ground. We surrender to you and are at your orders."

"Roger, Ferret," Tag responded. "Alpha Fox, any assault on the prisoners on the hill will be an act of aggression in violation of the cease-fire and will nullify that agreement. Ferret, we accept your surrender and give you leave to resist all actions against you by elements of the Warsaw Pact forces."

The air sang with silence.

Inside the No Slack Too, the crew sat agape at Tag's audacity, how he had forged a battlefield alliance in the face of two enemies. But none of them had escaped reality.

"Aw, fuck my uncle's duck," Fruits Tutti whined. "I'm fuckin' in love, Captain Max. Do we hafta do dis shit?"

And Ham Jefferson added, "Listen to the little man, Boss. I been in enough scraps to know when I'm overmatched."

Before Tag could respond, the air-alarm klaxon blared, and his radar screen came alive with blips, scattering like fleas on a griddle.

"Stealth," Tag said at once, recognizing the radar signature.

"Butcher Boy, Butcher Boy," an American voice said over the radio, "this is Dayhawk. I monitored your last. Do you need support? Over."

Tag figured it out at once. "Affirmative, Dayhawk. Can you put a load between—I say again, *between*—the two tank formations on south side of town? Over."

"Roger, Butcher Boy, if that's what you want. Dayhawk out."

Keying the Soviet frequency, Tag said, "Ferret, this is Butcher Boy, stand by to wheel right and follow me. Alpha Fox, inform your outposts not to oppose us."

Yeshev was furious at Tag's arrogance, and in the moment that he took to fume before responding, the earth exploded before him. His own radar had failed to detect even a false echo of the Stealth fighter-bomber formation that seemed to spring from the contour of the earth to the east, sowing a black rain of bombs and antitank mines along the length of the Soviet line.

Tag saw the bombs begin to blossom, blocking Yeshev's view of the defecting tanks behind a curtain of smoke.

"Ferret, this is Butcher Boy, turn and run," Tag ordered, then keyed his own TacNet and said, "Disciple, Lazarus, pick up these guys and take point, first alternate withdrawal route. I'll cover the six. Do you copy? Over."

Prentice and N. Sain confirmed Tag's message, and he ordered Wheels to hold their position until the others had cleared the knoll and were turning back north for a fast run up the open corridor out of Grabbe.

Keying the Soviet frequency a final time, Tag said, "Alpha Fox, this is Butcher Boy. See you around, sucker." Turning to Wheels, he said, "Kick it," and the XM-F4 spun from its fighting position and shot off to catch up with the rear of the escaping column.

As the No Slack Too raced along the centerline of the bypass toward the north side of Grabbe, a 2S9 from one of the flank elements of Yeshev's formation caught sight of it and sped through the deserted city streets to cut off the Americans. Emerging from the town and into the agricultural suburb on the north, the Soviet tank had a long stretch of the bypass under its gun and the No Slack Too was still in sight. Tag, who had been covering the town with his scope, saw the 2S9 when it came into view, saw its cannon begin to track, and shouted, "Stop," at the same instant that the Soviet fired, causing the round to pass inches from the muzzle of the No Slack Too's main tube.

"Target," Tag said. "Sabot."

"Confirmed," Ham replied.

"Shoot."

"Shot."

The penetrator core of the 120mm sabot struck just inside the right track of the compact tank, shearing the assembly off the chassis and perforating the men inside with the shrapnel of their own armor.

"Move," Tag said, and in another two minutes they had sighted the column and were out of cannon range of Yeshev's guns.

Even at the slower pace dictated by the captured Soviet armor, Tag's column made hot time along the road. By 1530 hours, he was able to order them back east, and by 1700 he was back in radio contact with the Jagd Kommando support center, where he arrived just before dusk.

8

Once his men were fed, billets found for the Soviets, and their vehicles secured by the Rangers, Tag sat down with Prentice and Giesla to review messages and put together an after-action report for command. The latest intelligence relayed by Colonel Barlow was that the First Guards army appeared to be redeploying to positions that would give them absolute command of the German shore of Lake Constance and a possible water-route for evacuation, if they could commandeer enough vessels to transport their tanks and heavy artillery. In fact, when all the factors were considered —the feasible landing sites, the areas of radiation, and the logistics—only one place on the east end of Lake Constance could possibly accommodate the Soviets' needs. It was a large bay with two ferry docks and a cargo facility and access to two highways and a rail line, from which a well-organized army could travel north and east along unoccupied high ground quite easily. Given the sparsity of NATO ground forces in the sector, the First Guards would have no effective opposition.

Tag tapped the map that they had spread on the farmhouse table, its corners held down with gas lanterns. "That pretty much tells the story, doesn't it?" he said. "My guess is that Barlow's gee-two is right on the money. Ivan knows that the route through Grabbe is compromised; the French are in the Black Forest; and everything else is a goddamn oven of radiation out there. But what we really need is to get in behind him, close enough for a solid read on the situation."

"What are you thinking, Max?" Giesla asked.

"I'm thinking this has to be fast and dirty, and the smaller the unit the better. Chuck, I'm leaving you and N. Sain and the Rangers all here. Especially now that we've got prisoners, I want enough bodies here to secure our rear. And if those Russian tankers have a change of heart, we'll need every one of you to keep them in line. Giesla, debrief those guys as best you can before Barlow sends somebody to get them."

"Tonight?" she asked.

Tag shook his head. "Tomorrow is soon enough. Give them a chance to get some rest and some hot chow."

"Max," Prentice said, "let me at least take one Bradley with you for backup. No troops, just me and a crew."

Tag said, "Forget it, Chuck. If it gets so bad that I need a Bradley for backup, a Bradley wouldn't be enough. Besides, I need you here."

"So," Giesla said, "what is the plan?"

"We'll overnight here, service the tank in the morning, and leave as soon as I have seen the early-bird pictures and cleared everything through Barlow. I want to make my final approach at night, anyway, so there's no rush. Chuck, set standard watches, plus a couple of guys on the Russians. Maybe you can even get something out of Ferret yourself. Me, I'm gonna take the night off."

When Prentice was gone and the maps put away, Giesla slipped her hand behind Tag's head and kissed him on the mouth.

"Max," she said, "I have missed you."

"You shouldn't worry about me," he said. "You have enough to do already."

Giesla cocked her head and smiled. "I did not worry, you thickhead," she said. "I said only that I missed you. I had time to do that, and I did."

Tag returned her smile. "And if I'd had the time, I would have missed you, too."

Giesla slipped from his arms and went to the cupboard, from which she took two glasses and a bottle of schnapps. "Get the lanterns and come along, Captain," she said, beckoning him with her head. "I have something for you that you will miss next time."

Holding a lantern in each hand, Tag followed her lithe figure out of the kitchen, up a steep flight of stairs, and into a hallway on the second floor. She stopped by an open door and said, "First, in here."

Tag held one of the lanterns through the door and saw the bathroom inside.

"Hot water," Giesla said, shifting the bottle and glasses to one hand and reaching for one of the lanterns, "and bath salts. Start the water, and I will come and wash your back."

"Where are you going?" Tag asked.

"Start the water," she said as she turned and crossed the hall and disappeared behind a door opposite the bathroom.

Tag opened the taps and dumped in a double handful of bath beads, letting the poaching-hot water fill the tub with suds and the air with steam, while he undressed and mused over how normal—not to say ordinary—his love for Giesla had become, how they could shut out the war and the world and live entirely within that love in the hours or minutes that were allowed to them. A head of foam was winking above the rim of the tub when Tag shut off the taps and slipped slowly into the suds.

His body had hardly adjusted to the heat of the water when Giesla returned, wrapped in a watered-silk kimono and carrying two glasses of schnapps. Over one arm she had draped another kimono of dark blue.

"Here," she said, handing Tag a glass and setting the other on a small table by the tub. "Drink this and give me some room." She shrugged off her kimono and hung it and the other one on a towel rack before stepping into the tub, facing Tag and easing herself into the water.

Tag took in her ankles, calves, thighs, hips, belly, and breasts as they disappeared beneath the head of foam. Her legs twined about his, and they stroked each other with their feet. They raised their glasses and drank.

"I take it back," Tag said. "I did miss you, I just didn't have time to realize it."

"Mmmm," she said, holding his foot and rubbing it between her high, full breasts, while simultaneously tickling the base of his balls with her toe. "You are a pig, Max Tag," she said. "Roll over and I will scrub that out of you."

Tag took another sip of schnapps, rolled over with his chin over the lip of the tub, and Giesla slithered up his back and began washing his shoulders with a thick cloth.

They washed and fondled each other for a half hour, taking occasional sips of schnapps, laughing at nothing, but hardly speaking until the foam began to die and the water turned tepid.

"All right," Giesla said as Tag gave her a last hard rub with one of the large towels from a stack in the bathroom cupboard. "Get dressed and come with me." She took the blue kimono off the rack and handed it to him.

Tag looked at the robe skeptically.

Giesla could not suppress a giggle. "Put it on," she said, "or I will tell everyone that you did."

She led Tag by the hand across the hall and into the bedroom, where she lit six candles standing on a plate and put out the lanterns. The bed was a deep eiderdown piled with pillows, and Giesla reclined on it languidly. "Pour me a drink, soldier," she said huskily.

Tag brought their drinks to the bed and stretched out beside her. Giesla raised her head and tossed off the schnapps in a single swallow, then let the glass roll from her fingers onto the rug. "Do not linger," she said, tugging at the knot on the sash of Tag's kimono.

He drank and dropped his glass on the other side of the bed. He parted Giesla's kimono and kissed his way from her face to her thighs, nuzzling in the creases where they joined her body, feeling the fine, curling hair of her bush against his cheek and smelling the sharp excitement of her sex. When he parted those lips with his tongue, Giesla gasped, then made a cooing sound in her throat as she stroked the back of his head. But after a few minutes, she could not wait.

"Come here, come here," Giesla said. She brought Tag's face to hers and guided him inside her with her other hand. "Oh, slow," she said. "As slowly as you can, Max."

They moved in a rhythm as strong and slow as
a deep river, and when they came it was like a
bursting of levees. And they broke many of them
before they slept.

The next morning was a full one for Tag. After
breakfast alone with Giesla, who had found fresh
eggs and real coffee for them, he rejoined his crew
and began preparations for their solo reconnaissance around Lake Constance. He ordered the
No Slack Too and the Bradleys decontaminated,
using an empty underground silo for a sump, and
encoded his after-action report for Colonel Barlow
while the vehicles were being foamed and hosed
down. The early-bird satellite photos and radar
images partially confirmed the information he had
about the Soviet movements, but they were not
conclusive. The new deployments could be taken
as an effort by the Soviets only to strengthen their
defensive position, in the event that the cease-fire
failed. Too, the more Tag thought about it, the
more he felt that the risks of attempting an evacuation on the lake, the vulnerability of an entire
army forced to use a single landing site, would
be greater than staying put and that the Soviet
commanders would recognize this. True, he told
himself, the First Guards army was cornered militarily and politically, and that might make them
desperate, but they were soldiers not sailors, and
even the prospect of facing fresh French troops in
the Black Forest would look better to most land
armies than the uncertainties of an unrehearsed
withdrawal by water. Of course, that could be just
what Ivan wanted them to think. More than ever,
it was clear that he had to find out the Soviets' real
intention and, if the lake was their choice, make
them reconsider.

By noon, the No Slack Too was ready, fully fueled and reloaded with ammunition, and Giesla had completed her preliminary interrogation of the Russian defectors. Aside from some confirming information about troop dispositions and critical shortages of supplies—made even more critical now that the army was cut off and Kettle was allowing no resupply—they knew even less than Tag about what was happening with the main body of the army to the south.

The sixty-odd kilometers to the lake was like a drive in the country. The fall colors were beginning to come out, and the day held the coolness of autumn. Skirting wide of any hot areas, Tag allowed the men to open all the hatches and take turns standing in the turret. Twice they encountered groups of civilians who were happy to hear that it was safe for them to move north and also provided Tag with useful information about conditions around the bay where he was headed. One of the ferries, he learned, had been scuttled and most, if not all, of the civilians in the area had fled weeks before. The docks, however, were intact, as his satellite photos had indicated, and there were many barges and small craft still in the slips.

Moving ever more slowly as they approached the lake, Tag ordered Wheels to leave the road and put them in a position where they could observe the entire bay while there was still light. From the cover of some abandoned vacation houses set on a rocky hill overlooking the water, Tag spent the last half hour of daylight combing the bay with his binoculars. Nearest to him, at the head of the bay, was the larger of the two ferry landings, with a large excursion boat sunk up to its decks only a few feet from the dock. Across the bay a car-passenger ferry that shuttled to the Swiss shore was still moored at the quay, and opposite it, to Tag's right, was the industrial port, with its warehouses and cranes. He counted three tugs and more than a dozen various scows and barges bobbing empty in the water, but no signs of human life.

"Hambone," Tag said to his gunner, once darkness had fallen, "get your gear and let's go have a look around."

While Ham checked his knives and slipped into the hand-tooled gangster rig that held his Colt 9mm and extra magazines, Tag slung on his own pistol harness and told Wheels and Fruits, "You guys hold the fort and keep your ears open. If you hear any shooting, come running. Things are just a little too quiet down there at the docks."

"Aye, aye, sir," Wheels said.

"And cut that Navy bullshit," Tag told him.

The moon was not yet up, and Tag and Ham had no trouble moving silently through the dark down to the port facility, a little more than a kilometer away. In addition to the featureless brick warehouse at the water's edge, there were two other buildings in the complex, one a dry dock or repair shop, with double train tracks running down into the water, and the other clearly an office building, a modern single-story structure with windows and a parking lot. Tag and Ham approached it first and found the front door locked.

"Feel like a little light B and E, Mister Jefferson?" Tag asked in a whisper. He could see Ham grin in the dark.

"Do I get to keep what I find?" Ham said.

The two men moved in a crouch below the level of the casement windows, until they found one slightly ajar. Ham took a short, thick-blade knife from his boot and quickly stripped the glazing putty from the lowest pane of the window, then slipped the blade through the crack between the frame and the jamb and pushed the glass out silently into his hand. Tag reached inside and cranked the window open.

Once inside the building, they waited and listened for a long minute before Tag risked a brief sweep around them with his miniature halogen flashlight, just enough for them to see that they were in a nondescript office full of filing cabinets. They crossed to the door, and Tag opened it slowly, relieved that its hinges were well-oiled and quiet and that the hallway beyond it was carpeted. Tag drew his Baretta, eased the safety off with his left hand, and started down the hall.

The corridor ran continuously from the reception area at the front of the building around the inside and back to the front again. All the doors leading off from it were shut, except for one that led into a windowless room in the center. With Ham covering him from the hall, Tag dropped to his belly and scuttled inside. There was not a sound, but in one corner he saw a small red light glowing on an electric coffee maker. Leaving Ham in the doorway, Tag rose and walked to the table where the coffee maker sat. Its glass carafe was half full of fresh java. In another minute, he had also located a vending machine full of snacks that had been pried open, a microwave oven, and a couch with blankets and a pillow piled on it. But whoever was living in the break room was not at home. He rejoined Ham at the door.

"Somebody has set up light housekeeping here, all right," he said. "Looks like just one. Let's go back the way we came and check out the warehouse."

The warehouse was easier to enter than the offices: its front door was standing open. From it, Tag and Ham could hear the sound of shoes on concrete echoing through the vast, empty space.

"So," Ham whispered, "what's the call?"

"Sounds like he's coming back this way," Tag said. "Let's go on in. You hang back a way and cover me, while I introduce myself. It's probably just a watchman or some such, but let's be careful and quiet."

"Quiet as a cat," Ham said. He palmed the handle of the slender Lile fighting knife on his thigh.

Just inside the door was a glassed-in office area. Tag and Ham waited by a corner of it until the footsteps were only a few feet away, then Tag stepped forward sensing more than seeing the outline of a figure in the dark. When he judged that the man was nearly close enough to touch, Tag switched on his halogen beam and aimed it where a face should have been. He never saw the face, however, because a tremendous concussion turned his whole world black.

Tag came to lying on the desk in the warehouse office. A fluorescent lamp turned toward the wall cast its glow over the faces of Ham Jefferson and a huge young man with a worried look, who stood looking down at Tag and wringing his hands. They were hands the size of dinner plates, with knuckles big as eggs, and were attached to a couple of the largest arms Tag had ever seen on a human. The boy—for he could hardly have been out of his teens, Tag decided—stood every inch of six and a half feet, easily weighed two-hundred fifty pounds, and didn't appear to carry an ounce of fat. When Tag tried to speak, he knew at once what had happened.

"Wha—," he began but flinched from the pain in his jaw and could not finish asking what he already knew. The boy was not only big but quick.

"I am sorry," the boy said, his voice surprisingly high and soft. "You are okay?"

"Mmmm," Tag grunted, trying not to move his jaw as he sat up. He hung his legs over the edge of the desk and massaged his cheek. "Good hit," he said from his throat.

"Just take it easy a minute, Boss," Ham said. "This is Peter, and we've been having a little talk while you took a nap. Want to hear the news?"

Tag nodded, and Ham went on.

"Well, Pete's folks, they own this place, and they had all cleared out, but he came back two days ago to keep an eye on things. Just last night, he says he saw what I guess were two amphibious tanks, like the ones the Soviet airborne uses. They came up into the bay, he says, and one of them came ashore here. A man got out, looked over the tugs and barges, and then they left. Now he's thinking maybe he should sink 'em or something—the barges, I mean. What about you?"

Tag moved his jaw gingerly. "Yeah," he said a little thickly, "sink me, too." He shook his head to clear it before he went on. "Well, if they were here in amphibs and looking over the vessels, that about clinches it." He thought for a moment, then said to the boy, "Peter, do you have anything floating out there that will carry thirty tons?"

"Oh, yes," Peter said. "Fifty metric tons, some of them."

Tag nodded. "OK, here's what we need. See if you can help us out. We need to load up a tank—an army tank, you know—and move it down the lake. And we need to do it tonight. Can we get a tank in one of those barges and tow it?"

The boy's face brightened. "Oh, better," he said. "A motor barge, we have, with a—a—"—he bent one of his massive arms like a policeman beckoning traffic.

"A ramp?" Tag said.

"Yes," Peter said. "One of those on the front. For tractors sometimes we carry."

"Ham," Tag said, "hiako back to the guys and get the No Slack Too down here. Peter, let's go have a look at your motor barge."

By the time Ham returned, Peter had nosed the barge up to the sloping shore near the dry dock and was showing Tag the controls in the open wheelhouse at the stern. He dropped the ramp and held the barge in position with the motor while Wheels pulled the XM-F4 into the cargo well, where only the tank's turret was visible above the gunwales. Tag would have liked to have camouflaged the turret, especially the unmistakable 120mm gun, but time and surprise were worth more to him now. He got Wheels out, introduced him to Peter, and left the two of them to go over the barge's controls, while he had a last look at their maps and had Fruits burp a message to Giesla that they were on the lake and moving to the west.

The quarter moon was just rising when Wheels piloted them into the bay. There was only the mildest of breezes moving over the water, and with the weight of the No Slack Too as ballast, the shallow-vee bottomed barge rode easily, its engine gratifyingly quiet at three-quarter speed as it pushed them along at four-and-a-half knots. Peter had taken obvious pride in telling Tag that with only thirty tons aboard, the barge was capable of six.

They were running a half kilometer out from shore and without lights, and Tag estimated that they could be well to the west of the Soviet positions within two hours, if all went as he hoped. He knew what they were doing was risky and hastily improvised, but with clear indications that Ivan was considering an evacuation up the lake, there was no purpose in fucking around overland. Even at that, he felt less anxiety about the hundred feet of water beneath him than he did about the prospect of accidentally stumbling into an entire Russian army while it was shifting positions in the dark. He scanned the water with his day/night binoculars and listened to the soft lapping against the blunt bow of the barge. Suddenly, he saw the moonlight rippling on the water nearer shore, drawn in vees by the wakes of six amphibious tanks.

He turned and called to the open cockpit in the stern, "Keep your head down, Wheels. We got bad guys in the water at two o'clock." Then he dropped down through the turret and set Fruits and Ham at battle stations.

Uncertain what the recoil of the 120mm would do, Tag told his gunner, "Bogeys at about two o'clock. You got 'em, Ham?"

"Dead in the water," Ham replied.

"OK, track 'em with the Phalanx. Maybe they won't see us, or maybe they won't be interested in a scow.

Tag heard the Phalanx barrels rotate once and the cupola hum as it followed the cross hairs Ham watched through his sight.

"What do you think, Boss?" Ham said. "Suppose they're going back to take over the port?"

"That'd be my guess. I just hope that kid Peter has enough sense not to take a swing at a tank."

"Uh-oh," Ham said. "Looks like somebody is interested in us after all."

Tag saw at once what he meant. Two of the six tanks had broken from the formation and were headed for the barge, whose entire right side was exposed to the amphibs' guns.

"Fruits," Tag said, "stick your head out and tell Wheels to bring us around head-on to these guys."

Midway through the barge's wallowing turn, something set off the Soviets' buzzer, and a hail of 12.7mm machine-gun fire swept the gunwales and pinged off the low turret of the No Slack Too.

"Nail 'em, Ham," Tag ordered, and the Phalanx shuddered to life.

Ham had already keyed both of the approaching tanks into the Phalanx computer, and the first round of the action was over in a matter of seconds. The initial burst of 37mm fire tore through the armor of the amphibious tank at the base of its turret and drove the nose down. Hundreds of gallons of water poured in behind the depleted-uranium slugs, sucking the tank down like a stone. But even before it was out of sight, its mate felt the fury of the Gatling-barreled Phalanx, as an almost solid skein of rounds bored through its exposed turret and set off an explosion that blew out through the hatches in gouts of orange flame, stark against the dark water.

Tag's sight of the remaining tanks was momentarily blocked by the explosion, and when he again had them in his scope, he saw that they were scattering, turning toward the barge and trying to envelop it.

Taking control of the Phalanx himself, Tag said, "Ham, main tube, HE round. Gunner's choice."

Operating on his own initiative, Wheels had brought the motor barge into a series of slow-motion maneuvers to prevent the amphibs from getting it in a cross fire. Tag spun the Phalanx cupola and raked two of the nearer swimming tanks, sending one of them into a list that became a capsize. The heavy machine guns on the three remaining tanks continued to pour a withering fire at the barge, puncturing its hull and sending ricochets off the No Slack Too whining inside the cargo bay. Calculating the possible results of recoil from the big gun, Ham fired the 120mm on manual and hit inches ahead of the most distant amphibious tank, blasting its nose up in a geyser of exploding water, lifting its treads out of the water. The tank came back down, wallowed as though negotiating a rutted road, then sank from sight. The recoil threw the barge into a violent pitch and roll that its nearly flat bottom did little to correct, throwing the horizon below the lip of the gunwale. With their roll back, Tag snapped off a short burst but was unable to confirm any hits. Before he or Ham could line up another shot, a tube-fired missile from one of the tanks struck forward on the barge, where the ramp met the hull, ripping a gaping hole that extended to just inches above the waterline and also giving Ham a line of sight for the 120mm. He triggered a round that obliterated the missile-firing tank in a cloud of smoke and steam, leaving a burning slick on the water where the tank had been.

The recoil from Ham's second shot caused the barge to rear back like a bucking horse, and when it slapped back down, lake water poured over the edge of the hole left by the missile in the bow. The weight of the water made the already unwieldy barge even more sluggish in its response to the tiller and slowed its speed, making it impossible for Wheels to pursue the lone fleeing amphibious tank.

"Check fire," Tag ordered, as he cut loose again with the Phalanx. Forced to aim and fire manually, he was successful only in wounding the tank, which slowed and began to trail a widening wake of oil but did not stop. The sheets of flaming fuel and oil on the surface of the lake, combined with the pitching and yawing of the barge, caused Tag to lose the tank in his IR sight. Realizing that the fight was over, he was out of the hatch at once to survey the damage.

Tag didn't know a lot about boats, but his first thought was that this one was staying afloat on imagination. The 12.7mm fire had perforated the hull in a hundred places, and the ricochets inside the cargo well had pocked it like a storm of mad hammers. Miraculously, Wheels was unhurt, despite a dozen holes through the wheelhouse.

"Oh, yeah, I'm okay, Cap'n," Wheels had said in response to Tag's shout. "But there's somethin' bad funky with these controls."

"Quarter in closer to shore," Tag said as he scrambled the length of the XM-F4's fender to get a look at the damage forward.

The sloshing water in the well came nearly to Tag's knees when he slid off the nose of the No Slack Too, and more was washing in with each pitching motion of the barge. It was impossible for Tag to tell whether the ramp was still operable, but that was the least of his worries at the moment. They were still nearly four-hundred meters from a shore where he wasn't sure they could land, even if they made it. They were taking on water, had a lame tiller, and were God only knew how close to the main body of the First Guards army. It was turning out to be a shitty night.

Back on top of the No Slack Too, Tag scanned the slowly approaching shore with his binoculars, their red cast throwing eerie shadows from the moonlight. At fifty meters from the bank, he had Wheels turn them parallel to it and move at slowest steerage speed, barely one knot. Then, just when Tag was beginning to seriously contemplate grounding the barge on whatever was nearest, he saw what he had been praying for. A wet-weather stream was running into the lake not a hundred meters ahead, and it had formed a sandy, rock-strewn delta where they could beach their craft and disembark the XM-F4—he hoped.

Shouting orders to Wheels, Tag piloted the balky barge toward the sloping shelf of the stream delta. The nose of the scow had hardly passed over the lip of the shallows when it began to slew to one side, and Wheels said, "Aw, shit, Cap'n, we lost it. I got no steerage."

"Drop the ramp," Tag called to him, "and get your butt back inside here." And with that, Tag himself scrambled down through the turret and into his own seat. He had the turbines humming when Wheels followed him inside moments later. He could feel the gentle flow from the stream pushing against the becalmed barge, nudging it back toward deeper water.

"Get us out of here," he said to his driver.

"All right," Wheels said, "but that ramp is only about halfway down."

Wheels slammed the No Slack Too into reverse and rammed the jammed ramp. It gave, stuck again, and the XM-F4 clawed its way up until its weight got the better of the contest, and the ramp collapsed with a crash and a ripping of steel. Water flooded over the rear deck of the tank, but Wheels never relaxed his demands on the throttles. The tracks found the bottom and jerked the No Slack Too free of the barge, pushing it away. As the No Slack Too came up into the shallows, the barge slipped away from shore and settled slowly beneath the surface of the lake with a gurgle of dying diesels.

Tag was working feverishly at his VDT, calling up map details to find a way out of here for them, when the air-alarm klaxon blared in the crew compartment, and Ham announced the presence of two helicopters.

"Hinds, maybe Havocs," the gunner said. "Coming in low."

Tag was in no mood for a sporting fight.

"Key War Clubs," he said as he switched his own screen to the air radar and confirmed the signatures of the rotary-wing aircraft.

"Two targets locked," Ham said.

"Shoot," Tag said, and a pair of the needle-nose missiles sizzled from their clamshell farings on either side of the turret.

The downward-looking radar on the two Mi-28 Havoc helicopters was searching for whatever it was on the surface of the lake that had destroyed the amphibious tanks, and the Soviet pilots had no warning before the deadly missiles hit them. Almost simultaneously, the pair exploded in mid-air, consuming their own magnesium-alloy skins in a falling inferno that lit the lake like gigantic flares in the instant before it swallowed them.

"Straight up the streambed, Wheels," Tag said. "We need a minute to sort this deal out."

Wheels whipped the XM-F4 about in the current by the shore and gunned the tank into the face of the flow.

9

Because it was not an outright lie, Yeshev was convincing to General Tsarchev when he reported that the garrison at Grabbe had been lost in an attack by Stealth fighter bombers. He was even more fortunate that the report of the fight on the lake came through while he was still being debriefed. And with the subsequent loss of the two Havocs only minutes later, all attention was directed away from him by the command group. Almost by instinct, Yeshev knew what must have been the source of the destruction. With something akin to elation, he thought, *So, Butcher Boy is coming to me.*

In the midst of activity that Tag and the No Slack Too had stirred up in the headquarters of the First Guards Tank Army, Yeshev said to General Tsarchev, "Comrade General, if the tank that was in that barge on the lake is the one I believe it is, it would be futile to pit any more of our light armor or conventional tanks against it. I have four T-80Bs in addition to my own. May I suggest that they be deployed to track down and destroy the American?"

Tsarchev paused a moment, then said, "Yes, Colonel, but I want you to lead them yourself. Intelligence will provide you whatever you need from them. But let me remind you, Colonel Yeshev, that this American—if it is who you say—is of maximum importance to me and to you. Maximum importance. Do you understand me?"

"Yes, Comrade General," Yeshev replied. "I understand perfectly."

Tag studied the maps and weighed their situation. On the downside, they were in lousy field position. To the south was the lake, and the shore immediately to the east and west was far too rugged for maneuvering, probably impassable, and just a few kilometers to the north was the frontier of the dead zone, an almost total stain of red on the radiation scale. The sole route open to them led northwest, directly into the teeth of the First Guards. What's more, with all the shuffling of that army, he had no way of knowing exactly where the Soviets now were and could not know before morning, providing that there was not too much radiation static here for the satellite pictures to come through. About the only good news was that Ivan didn't know where he was either, but he had to assume that there would be patrols or even air recon out looking for them.

"Okay, sweethearts," he said to the crew, "we got nothing but buffalo chips to eat, but we got plenty of them. Wheels, look at the map I'm putting on your screen. Seems to be a stand of timber in that rough country about a klick and a half to the northwest. Put us in there. Ham, Fruits, all systems up. Sabot in the main tube. And everybody keep their fingers crossed."

Wheels touched his controls, and the powerful XM-F4 scrambled up and out of the creek gully, into a barren, rocky stretch of the plateau that was virtually uninhabited and contained no major roads. Behind them to the east were the lush hills of timber and dairy farms, and farther to the east the picturesque terraced vineyards and orchards that lined much of the north shore of Lake Constance. But here in the margin between them was little except hard ground, semialpine scrub, and steep erosion ravines. For the No Slack Too, it was good ground for making fast time.

Within fifteen minutes, Wheels had brought them to the complex of razorback ridges with their stands of gnarled oak, where Tag found a place he liked on the high ground.

"Here's the drill, guys," he said, once they were in position. "We're going to have to make a run through Ivan's formation. Only problem is we don't know exactly where that is, not with all the redeployment that's been going on. And he's going to be looking for us at the same time. We've got speed, and we've got surprise, and we know more about where he is than he knows about us. For now, I want us all to get some rack. One-man watches. We'll roll at zero-four-hundred."

Yeshev lost no time in assembling his scratch squadron of T-80Bs. He had handpicked each commander and crew personally, and he had no doubt that they represented the very best in tanks and men that the Warsaw Pact forces could put in the field. He had roused Nikolai Viktor and put the intelligence officer to work piecing together everything he could to help pinpoint the location of the American tank, but what was available was little and nothing. Tsarchev had allowed him two light helicopters to fly reconnaissance, and they had confirmed that there was nothing afloat on the lake that might contain Butcher Boy, but that was hardly news, and even with the lake eliminated from his search, it was nearly 0200 before he had an epiphany, one of those unbidden insights that had become the hallmark of his tactical genius.

Butcher Boy was aggressive, even audacious, and if he survived the battle on the lake, as Yeshev felt confident he had, he must have come ashore near where it occurred. Coming to many of the same conclusions about terrain and limitations imposed by the nuclear red areas that Tag had, Yeshev saw at once what his adversary must be planning. It worried the Soviet tanker that he did not know how good Tag's intelligence was, how much he knew about the First Guards' dispositions and movements, but if the American was intending to move through their formations, the topography limited him to three or possibly four routes. That was all Yeshev needed. Infantry pickets along each route would be his eyes and ears, and he could then hold all of his T-80Bs in a single location for a fast-reaction strike.

Yeshev sent out the orders for the infantry outposts, then had the best few hours sleep he had enjoyed in many nights.

Tag awoke in his commander's chair feeling stiff and unrested. Fruits Tutti, who had taken the last watch in the driver's seat, handed him a cup of instant coffee and said, "Pretty short night, huh, Captain Max?"

Tag sipped the tepid coffee, made a face, and said, "Yeah, and this shit would make a blind man lame. Anything shakin'?"

"Nothin' I could see, Cap. I had somethin' on the audio locator about a half hour ago, motor noise, like a truck, maybe a coupla klicks to de northwest."

"Just one, Fruits?"

"Yeah. It was behind dem next rises, couldn't get no visual fix. But it sounded like just one. Came, stopped, and turned around and went back. Coulda been anything."

"You got that right, Mister Tutti. Roll those other apes out of the turret, and let's go check it out."

It took the crew only ten minutes to piss, choke down some of the bitter coffee and reconstituted eggs, and be rolling again. Tag ordered the turbines baffled down into whisper mode and halted the No Slack Too below the crest of the rise beyond which Fruits had heard the truck. He grabbed his day/night binoculars and crawled to the top.

It took a few minutes for Tag to locate the squad of Soviet infantry strung out in the ditches on either side of the road at the foot of the rise and even longer to get an inkling of why they were there.

"Wheels," Tag said as he dropped through the commander's hatch, "Ivan is stringing infantry trip wires, and we've got one across the road down there. Think you can handle those gullies just north of here?" He brought up the map detail on the driver's screen.

"Well," Wheels drawled, "it ain't no day at the beach, but I reckon we can handle it. If you're not in any hurry, that is."

"Just do it."

Still running at a whisper, the No Slack Too traveled parallel to the rise until a saddle in its crest allowed Wheels to traverse it without profiling them against the horizon. Then he cut directly down the opposite slope, crossed the road more than a kilometer from the infantry position, and threaded his way into a crosshatch of dry gullies and runoff streams that had forced the road builders to swing to the south. It was a bone-crunching and laborious passage, but in thirty minutes they had negotiated it, and Tag turned them back south to pick up the road.

"Gentlemen," he said as they gathered speed along the macadam, "from here it gets tricky. Ivan at least has a hunch that we're still out here —somewhere—and he's everywhere, so there's no point in getting cute. Just this side of Meersburg there's a highway that hooks back toward the dead zone. We'll have Ivan between us and home, but we can go places he can't. We're going to go flat out for it and just pray we don't run up the six of their HQ, because, I tell you, I don't have a clue where all the bad guys are right now."

"Maybe we oughta wait on the early bird, Captain Max?" Fruits Tutti asked.

"I thought of that, Fruits, but those pictures won't be coming down until after first light, and we need to do as much as we can in the dark. We've got about another hour, so let's get busy. Wheels, open the baffles."

Wheels shifted the No Slack Too to full power, and the low black tank shot forward like a sprinter out of the blocks. In ten seconds it had topped one hundred kilometers per hour and in another ten was running wide open at nearly one hundred and fifty. When it passed the second infantry pickets five klicks down the road, the Soviet soildiers had to hold a debate to decide what they had seen.

•   •   •

It was 0520 when Yeshev got the word that
the Americans had passed one of his outposts,
and his crews were ready to respond. Taking the
point himself, Yeshev laid a course for the ten
kilometers they had to cover to intercept the No
Slack Too, and the five massive T-80Bs roared
away in column. His only concern was that one
of the infantry antitank units that he had also
ordered to respond would neutralize the Americans before he got there.

The first pale light was breaking behind them
when Tag and his men hit the first Soviet ambush.
Two BRMs full of antitank commandos had fallen
out just moments before and deployed themselves
and their arrays of ATGMs at a crossroads just
five kilometers from Meersburg, but not knowing
it was an XM-F4 that they were hunting, the
Warsaw Pact troops were unprepared for what
hit them.

The No Slack Too seemed to spring from nothing. With its twin turbines pushed past their red
line, the tank came on them like a cyclone, and
the soldiers' first rounds went wild, as a pair of
their missiles converged on a spot on the road
where the No Slack Too had been a full second
before.

Tag saw the heat signatures of the rockets' igni-
tion on his screen an instant before they flashed
past and ruptured the pavement behind him.

"Fruits, take the Phalanx," he shouted as he
swung his own coaxial 7.62mm into action.

Small-arms and machine-gun fire swarmed the
No Slack Too like frustrated gnats as it closed
on the Soviet position faster than most of the

gunners could follow. Tag lay down a searing
fire from his light-machine gun, walking rounds
down the roadside in long bursts that chopped
holes in the lines of the enemy infantry, while
Fruits locked on targets with the IR/Doppler-
laser sight and spit controlled salvos of 37mm
destruction at the Communist missile stands.
Despite the fury and accuracy of the Americans'
counterfire, there were too many targets for Tag
and Fruits to neutralize without stopping. One,
two, three direct hits from the ATGMs battered
the No Slack Too as it covered the last hundred
meters to the crossroads. The slick-skin armor and
slippery lines of the XM-F4 turned them, but the
walloping impacts staggered the tank, and Wheels
had to fight his controls to maintain their course,
like a bomber pilot juking through heavy flak. The
last hit they took from the missiles caromed off
the turret, shearing away the mini-gun mount and
antenna array.

Fruits spun the Phalanx cupola as they passed
between the legs of the Soviet ambush, blasting
men and missile racks into the air in a lethal
contusion of flesh and steel. Not a half dozen of
the enemy were left alive, and both of the BRMs
stood in flames, their tires bursting from the heat.

"Systems check," Tag called out, already aware
that their ComNet communications were shot.

"Strack," came all three replies.

No question now, Tag thought, *the chase is on
for real.*

Regardless of what he knew or suspected about
the capabilities of the American tank, Yeshev
could not suppress a feeling of urgency when the
report from the survivors of the infantry ambush

came through to him. The Americans had not
only run headlong through the ambush and
survived direct hits from AT-Bs that would have
annihilated an Abrams or a standard T-80, they
had also wiped out the ambush in the process.
Any hope he had that the infantry might at least
slow or detour his quarry was put aside entirely.
He would not call off the other infantry units
that even now were rushing to take up positions
along the route of the No Slack Too, but his last
remaining confidence was in the T-80Bs and his
own skill. He was less than five kilometers from
the Meersburg highway and could almost feel
the texture of the battle that he was shaping in
his mind, the way an athlete visualizes victory
before the event. This, he knew, was identical
to the quasi-mystical approach to victory that
his war college professors had scoffed at in Ross
Kettle's writings, but he knew, too, that it worked.
Yeshev ordered two of his tanks to peel away
from the column and take a short angle on the
Meersburg road, while he drove the remainder of
the column toward his primary fighting position
on the northern outskirts of the town.

Random shots from everything from AK-74s to
RPGs to antitank cannons made up the gauntlet
the No Slack Too had to run as it raced along the
final kilometers to the Meersburg road. Twice
there were hasty roadblocks thrown up—trucks
and light four-wheel-drive command cars run
haphazard across the highway, but they proved
no real obstacles. The first appeared suddenly,
just over a rise in the road, and Wheels had
time only to choose a seam and hit it at full
throttle, scattering the vehicles like toys and

sending the men behind them spinning crazily
through the air in pinwheels of shattered flesh
and bone. At the second, Wheels showed a trace
of his old blockade-running skills as he banked
the XM-F4 up a high berm around the clot of
five-ton trucks and came skidding back onto the
pavement, fishtailing out of the maneuver and
regathering his speed all at once.

Realizing that the Soviets had recognized his
route, Tag ordered his driver to veer off the road
less than a kilometer from its intersection with
the Meersburg highway and cut through a grid of
access roads that served a small industrial park
outside town. It cost him some precious seconds,
but Tag had no desire to press their luck. Already
the No Slack Too had absorbed more than its due
of heavy hits, and any one of them could have
struck a tread or hatch seam, the most vulnerable
points on the tank.

There was no road or street connecting the
industrial park directly with the highway running
north–northeast out of Meersburg, so Tag and
his men had to take to the open country in
between, while long-shot projectiles from BMPs
and a single T-64B stationed in the town whizzed
around them, gouging craters in the open fields
to no effect on the No Slack Too as it screamed
through the matrix of explosions and singing steel.
Wheels cleared a shallow stream that cut across
the fields in a single leap, and the XM-F4 bounced
on its air-torsion suspension, springing forward as
though ready to leave the ground. At the same
time, Ham returned fire on the lighter armor in
the town with a succession of HE rounds that
sent the BMPs and the T-64B scuttling in retreat
among the stone houses. The lethal reputation of

the No Slack Too had already spread among the enemy.

Yeshev could hear the sound of the guns, although at two kilometers away and screened by the dips and rises of the Meersburg road, he could not yet see the battle. He took the high ground of one rise himself and lay the other two T-80Bs on either side of the road, where all three of their fields of fire would converge on the approaching slope, hoping for a shot from above the American tank. Unless its design were a grand departure from anything he knew, the top of the turret and the rear deck should prove least heavily armored, and his tube-fired Tree Toad missiles could put an end to things once and for all.

From the next to last rise before the depression where Yeshev hoped to catch him, Tag spotted a fragment of a T-80 profile on the horizon of the road ahead.

"Wheels," he said, "left, off the road. Heavy armor dead ahead. Ham, sabot."

Wheels cried, "Bumps," as he cleared the ditch parallel to them, crashed through a wire fence, and swung out into the cleared right of way. But there was only so far he could go, for the edge of the easement was bound by a dense stand of second-growth evergreens.

Careening at high speed over the crazily angled lay of the land, Ham worked feverishly to keep his gun in effective attitude. Rounding the shoulder of the rise, he had one of the flanking T-80Bs directly in front of him and touched off the sabot on reflex.

The integral-propellant round roared from the pitching tube and struck low and to the rear on the Soviet tank, destroying its drive carriage and engines, which burst into flame. An answering shot from the other flanker whistled wide, but there the No Slack Too's luck ran out.

In the moment that the No Slack Too's forward motion was checked by the recoil of its own gun, Yeshev's less sophisticated laser sight locked on it, and a latest-generation Tree Toad flared from the tube of the T-80B. The armor-piercing warhead of the missile was designed for use against reactive armor, its effect coming by being able to withstand the back blast of the reactive cassettes and make an adhesive puddle that would hold for the split second it took for the heat of its charge to burn through 300mm of steel-and-glass composite. The slick-skin armor on the No Slack Too was far superior to the composite, but the microns-thin seam at the hatches was not.

The Tree Toad struck at a steep angle at the lip of the driver's hatch, most of its cutting-torch effects melting a shallow seam across the skin, but enough force found its way into the seam to blast its way into the crew compartment.

Yeshev observed the impact with satisfaction, saw the black low-slung tank veer and shudder, then race up the hill at unbelievable speed while firing again at the surviving flanker and scoring a hit that tore the entire upper third off the T-80B's boxy turret. He called out to his own gunner for another Tree Toad, but his order was drowned and the awkward manual loading of the missile interrupted by a covering burst from the Phalanx that tattooed his tank like a jackhammer. When he recovered, the Americans were past him, back on the road, and gone from sight.

Yeshev radioed his two remaining tanks that the No Slack Too was coming, then wheeled about and again took up the chase, certain that the American tank was wounded and that it was now just a matter of minutes until it was his.

The initial impact of the Tree Toad staggered the No Slack Too, temporarily stalling one of its turbines, and in the next instant there was a crack, like a pistol shot as white-hot fragments of armor and missile exploded above Wheels Latta's head. The driver screamed in pain and slumped back in his seat, wrapping his body in both arms.

Tag had no time for anything but to grab the controls, jab the restart button, and shout, "Shoot, shoot," as he ran for his life, for all their lives, from the deadly cross fire. He didn't even know that he was hit.

Tag would never know whether it was minutes or seconds before he felt the pain, stiffness, and blood, but all at once he realized that his right shoulder was not working, and we was losing grip strength on the controls.

"Wheels, Wheels," he said, fighting down the adrenaline that choked his voice, "are you hurt? How bad are you hurt?"

"I got it. I got it, Cap'n," Wheels said. But in a glance, Tag could see that the driver had not moved. He still had himself wrapped up as though against a chill, and the whole front of his NBC suit was a dark stain of red spreading down into his lap.

"Fruits," Tag said over the intercom, "get the medical kit down here. Wheels is hit."

Agile as a monkey, the wiry loader sprang down from the turret and tilted back the driver's chair. Without a word or an instruction, he pulled Wheels's arms away from his body, slit open his suit, and doused his chest and belly with peroxide and water. Wheels Latta was bleeding heavily from a dozen pea-size wounds in a massive bruise that covered his entire torso.

"Aw, jeez," Fruits said softly. He covered his friend's body with large wound pads and tied battle dressings across them, cut through the fabric on his upper thighs and dressed several smaller wounds in them, then popped Wheels with a quarter-grain styrette of morphine and uncoiled a sterile needle and tube from a foil packet of blood extender that he hung from the handle of the damaged hatch above him.

"How bad?" Tag asked.

"Plenty," Fruits said. "Aw, jeez. Yeah, plenty."

"Do what you can," Tag said, "then get back in your seat. We're not out of the woods yet."

Yeshev was stunned by the speed of the No Slack Too. Even at his T-80B's top end of more than one hundred and ten kilometers per hour, he was still losing ground on the Americans. He radioed his two tanks that were in blocking position, telling them to take good cover and to be ready for something moving faster than any tank they had ever seen. The dips and rises in the road prevented him from getting a clear shot, and he did not dare stop on top of one and lose any more distance for the mere chance at a shot. At last, he fully realized that he was in combat with the very embodiment of Ross Kettle's vision of tank warfare, and he felt a grudging but very deep and very real respect for this enemy, a fond sadness that he had to be destroyed.

Tag brushed off Fruits's offer to treat his wounded shoulder and kept his eyes glued to his screens and commander's scope, anything to keep from looking at Wheels. As he brought the No Slack Too over another rolling ridge, he saw ahead the secondary road splitting off to the right that would give him the shortest route back to the Jagd Kommando command center—a route that led in part through the blood-red blot of most intense nuclear destruction and radiation. Instinctively searching the intersection for possible ambush sites, he also saw the fighting position of one of the awaiting T-80Bs. He locked it in his sights.

"Target," Tag announced. "Sabot."

"Confirmed," Ham responded.

"Shoot."

"Shot."

The No Slack Too reared as it ran, and the 120mm tube collapsed back on its dampers and recovered. The sabot penetrator nicked the top of the earthen ditch bank that the T-80B had gone behind for cover, causing a puff of dust that Tag saw in what looked like slow motion before the Soviet tank jerked with internal explosions and black smoke started to uncoil from the intake stacks on its rear deck.

That one's for you, Wheels, he thought, but he did not have time to relish the revenge. The other T-80B, fighting from the thick concealment of the roadside evergreens, loosed its own sabot, striking the knife-edge fender of the No Slack Too and peeling back three feet of it, exposing the track, before detonating in a ringing explosion just aft of the turret.

Fruits Tutti marked it with the Phalanx, aiming at the smoke, and slashed the young timber with the maxi gun. The Soviet tank's improved composite armor turned the initial burst, giving its commander time to lurch his machine forward into a defile and out of the sights of the awesome cannon.

"Keep the motherfucker's head down, Fruits," Tag said. "We're gonna hang a right."

Tag barreled down the highway and made a hard turn onto the secondary road, passing less than one-hundred meters from the surviving Soviet, while Fruits kept up a rhythmic pulse of covering fire with the Phalanx. Tag didn't know how far the Soviets might pursue him into the dead zone, for these were certainly not conventional T-80s he was dealing with, nor did he know how long he could go without patching the thumb-size hole in the hatch before radiation began to funnel through it. Worst of all, he didn't know if he could go on losing blood from his now-useless right arm and shoulder and still command the tank, or whether any of them would make it through the dead zone if he did.

When Yeshev topped the rise above the inter-section, the No Slack Too was a receding smudge on the road to the atomic wasteland. He took in the scene at once, and his heart sank. Another of his prized T-80Bs sat in ruin, now aboil in inky smoke, while the other only now was emerging from hiding, its heretofore courageous commander a nearly broken man. Yeshev had seen enough of the American tank to know that they had no hope of catching it. He sat and watched it disappear. He well knew where that road led, and he was sure that the Americans would not be turning back. He was sick at heart over the loss of his men and the tanks of which he had been so proud, but his sense of defeat was greater than that. Deep in his bones he knew that, regardless of anything the general staff or General Tsarchev might do, regardless of how well he continued to fight, this war was over.

Yeshev rolled slowly down the grade and radioed for help in picking up the dead.

10

Wheels Latta was dead, all his courage and skill
stilled with the heart that pumped out his life
through a score of ragged wounds.

When it was clear to Tag that the Soviets
would not pursue him, he halted the No Slack
Too and found his driver dead. He told Ham and
Fruits, and the three of them wrapped Wheels in
a poncho, laid him in the back of the turret, and
secured the body with cargo straps. None spoke
or even noticed the others' tears. Those were for
another time. Tag at last allowed Fruits to dress
his wounded shoulder, which was mauled and
swollen by the fragments and virtually useless.
He hurt terribly but refused any morphine.

The Tree Toad missile that had killed Wheels
and wounded Tag had bored a molten channel
through the seam between hatch and deck and
welded the locking dogs in place. Ham packed
the hole with a fast-drying resin that swelled to
fill the irregularities and hardened in minutes to
form a secure NBC seal. A quick inspection of
the damage from their running battle revealed the
loss of the mini-gun and the antenna array, leaving
them with only their TacNet. The fender that had
been ripped back by the sabot from the T-80B was
an ugly thing, all twisted angles and sharp edges,

and it exposed a portion of the track and carriage, but it did not otherwise affect the performance of the No Slack Too. There were hundreds of smaller dents and pings in the slick-skin armor. All critical systems, however, were intact and operable. Tag ordered the main tube plugged at the muzzle, applied resin around the gun-mantle boots, and had all the ventilation filters replaced. Everyone changed into fresh NBC suits and attached their gas masks to the breather port.

At 1000 hours, they were as ready as they could be to hazard the heart of the nuclear-strike zone.

Tag settled himself gingerly into his seat, his shoulder throbbing. "If either of you remember any prayers," he said to Ham and Fruits, "now would be a good time to dust them off."

"What's it look like up ahead, Bossman?" Ham asked.

"Like hell on Earth, Hambone. I'd estimate forty or fifty nukes blanketed the area; it's where the main concentrations of Ivan's nuclear artillery and missile launchers were located, along with a division or so of ground troops. We'll be the only things alive in there, and we won't be staying long. But I want all of us to stay on the scopes and make videotapes. There'll be some important gee-two come out of all this, and we're not going to let Kettle miss it."

"So, we're gonna make it, huh?" Fruits said.

"We're gonna make it, Fruits," Tag replied, wishing he believed it. "Now, let's tear it up."

Tag had plotted the most direct course he could that would still allow them to avoid plowing through any ground-zero points—but not by much, for in places there were lines of impacts that fell less than a kilometer apart. He didn't think it was necessary to point that out to his crew, however. He revved the turbines, engaged the transmission, and accelerated smoothly to one hundred kilometers per hour.

In five minutes the radiation count outside began to climb, and within fifteen it was higher than anything they had yet had to endure, almost 300 RADs. There was no picking their way through this; everything was hot, and the road at least kept them moving through it quickly. Inside the sealed off XM-F4, the highest radiation levels came from the VDT screens.

Tag had no intention of slowing down just to get better shots on the video recording he was making for intelligence, piping images from his sights and various electronic viewing devices into the VCR, but what he could see gave him another sort of pause. Passing just 1,500 meters from the center of the blast area that marked the beginning of the red zone, he sighted the remains of a Soviet artillery emplacement that he at first mistook for a scrap and reclamation center. The earthworks around the gun pits and FDC center were all that remained of man's work on the landscape, scorched and vitrified parapets that lay like neolithic giants' rings upon the harrowed earth. The caissons of the guns were amorphous lumps and the barrels drooping caricatures. The kind of heat necessary to generate such obliteration was not imaginable to Tag, and what he took to be miscellaneous debris he finally realized were the carbonized bodies of Warsaw Pact soldiers. What had been trees now lay like radiating shadows on the ground, pointing accusingly toward the source of their destruction. And this was only the beginning.

Much of the topography in this quarter of the German state of Baden-Württemberg, bound by the Danube and Iller rivers and lying southwest of them, reminded Tag of the Ozark plateau of Missouri and Arkansas before it rises into the steep ridges of the mountains proper. Mostly rolling country that had been cleared and turned to dairy farming and fruit crops, it was punctuated by irregular formations of rugged hills that had been left wooded. Streams flowed from them to water the arable land below. Now those hills were covered in forests of standing ashes, save for the tops, which had been swept clean by the blasts and gave the hills the look of surreal volcanoes.

The road they were traveling took several twists and turns around and through these hills and in places was itself blistered and buckled by the heat, causing Tag to have to slow their progress. In one atomic defile, between two impacts that had occurred less than a kilometer apart, the road was practically consumed, and he had his best—or worst—illustration of what nuclear war was really about.

All about him, Tag could see the blackened and twisted carcasses of tanks, trucks, and self-propelled artillery pieces, most of them identifiable only by some scrap of chassis or body that retained a semblance of its original configuration. There was no order to them, no arrangement that would suggest how they might have been deployed or where. In places they were fused together into windrows of steel, and in others they were simply scattered like toys thrown in spite by a petulant child. The surface of the ground had the scoured look of a glacial moraine, though in place of rocks there were parts from machines

and unrecognizable pieces of military gear. Eeriest
of all, however, was a steel tower, whose function
Tag could not guess, that had somehow remained
standing. Black and skeletal, it stood alone, far
from any obvious military position, the tallest
thing on the landscape.

The radiation readings outside the tank had
climbed off the charts of the instruments on the
No Slack Too, but inside, the count was just a
fraction above normal. Tag felt his first tug of deep
grief for Wheels Latta, and that combined with
his realization that they had just ten kilometers
to go until they were out of the dead zone gave
him a confidence that they really would make it.
He didn't know whether enough of the radiation-
absorbing polymer on the skin of the No Slack Too
had survived to make decontaminating it feasible,
but he knew now that they could survive.

Tag's mixture of grief and relief did not last
long. As the only thing moving on the landscape,
the No Slack Too stood out starkly to the pilots
of the two high-flying MiG-31s. They were the
last of the fixed-wing aircraft left with the First
Guards, and their permission to overfly the dead
zone was nothing less than a coincidence. Their
orders were only to evacuate certain secret documents and return to their combat base in Bavaria
before it was retaken by the NATO armies once
the cease-fire was lifted. But the pilots, too, had
heard the tales of the American tank and how
it alone had disrupted the Grand Gambit. Now
spotting it alone and in the open, the lead
pilot elected to risk his mission for revenge
and personal glory. He armed the missiles on
his weapons pods and banked into an attack
attitude.

The air-alarm klaxon shattered Tag's thoughts, and his radar screen leapt to life.

"Fixed wing," he cried. "Arm War Clubs. Phalanx on robotic response."

The turret and the Phalanx cupola rotated independently, each drawing a bead on the swooping MiG.

The pilot of the MiG-31 was confused. He had the tank in his visual sight, and his radar system showed continuity, but the blip on his screen kept breaking up, confusing the guidance systems in the noses of his missiles, as the Stealth coating on the No Slack Too absorbed and deflected his radar beams. Undaunted, the Soviet pilot pushed his stick forward, determined not to break off his attack. And he might have succeeded, if he had not left the radar on.

"Shoot one," Tag ordered, and the War Club that leapt from the faring rode the MiG's radar beam toward the sky.

Flying solo, without a systems officer, the pilot realized too late what he had done. He snapped a half-roll, trying to pull out of his dive, and released a canister of foil confetti that had no time to burst and confuse the antiaircraft missile before it collided with his jet and turned it into a winged, tumbling ball of fire. The circling wingman made a better choice and kicked in his afterburners on a course for home.

"Splash and burn," Tag said.

"Damn," Ham said, "don't these suckers ever quit?"

"I think they're learning, Ham," said Tag. "I really do. All we can do is keep teaching 'em the same lesson over and over."

"Hey, Captain Max," Fruits piped in, "can we let school out, just for a while?"

"Hang onto your hats," said Tag, and he booted up the throttles.

By the time the RAD count began to drop back into the range of their instruments, Tag knew he was, in his own mind, home free: the pain in his shoulder had become almost too much to bear. Sweat was standing in marbles on his forehead and upper lip, and he was feeling sick to his stomach. At a swollen creek only minutes from the intersection with their original route down to the lake, he plunged the No Slack Too into a deep pool and let the current flush away any loose radioactive dust they had collected, while he caught his breath and decided he could risk a shot of morphine.

Fruits clambered down from the turret, unzipped Tag's NBC suit, and administered a styrette of painkiller in his commander's good arm.

Tag had forgotten the effects of the opiate on a man in pain. He felt no elation, no giddiness, not really any cessation of the pain, only a distancing of it, an ability to put it aside and get on with what was at hand. But he had not forgotten that this would last only three hours or so, yet that would be all he would need.

Tag pulled the No Slack Too out of the creek and back onto the road. Within a quarter-hour, they were entirely out of the dead zone and its penumbra of fallout, riding fast toward the Jagd Kommando support center. In another ten minutes, they were within range of the TacNet and announced their arrival with a caution that they were coming in hot.

Even on such short notice, Giesla was able to clear the area around the underground silo that was their nuclear dump and had the solvents and the pressure washer ready to decontaminate the No Slack Too. She directed Tag onto the ramped end of the silo, and N. Sain, Mad Dog, and Rabies, who had volunteered for—no, insisted on—the duty, brought the equipment up and hosed down the tank. After an hour of solvents, foam, and soapy water, the XM-F4 was as clean as field procedures could make it, and Tag and his men could come out.

Fruits and Ham refused any help in removing Wheels's body from the turret and would allow no one else to touch it until they had laid their dead comrade out, said some words over him alone, and composed themselves enough to rejoin Tag.

Giesla had been the first one to him when he emerged from the tank. At once, she saw the wad of battle dressings on his shoulder and the morphine glaze of his eyes and called for Bones, the medic. When Ham and Fruits came up, she left Tag sitting in the seat of her Kommando car, where Bones was treating him, and went to meet them.

Giesla opened her arms to the black gunner and his gnomelike loader, and they both embraced her at once. None of them felt the need to speak for the many beats of their sad hearts. At last Giesla said, "I thank God you are both well. You are my brothers now. Come with me."

With the wisdom of women and good commanders, she fed them fresh food and gave them hot coffee with schnapps, then found something for them to do. Fruits she sent to retrieve the videotape of their passage through the dead zone, and Ham she told to supervise the refueling and rearming of the No Slack Too. Then she returned to check on Tag.

Tag sat with his head back on the seat, his eyes slightly glassy with pain, stress, and morphine, while Bones picked shrapnel from his shoulder and blotted up the blood with a battle dressing. Giesla had to avert her eyes from the bruised and swollen flesh. She went to the other side of the car, sat in the driver's seat next to Tag, and took his good hand in her own.

Before she could find any words, Tag said, "You get anything else out of those Russians?" His voice was flat and distant.

Instinctively, Giesla knew what Tag was going through. When her own brother, Heinrich, had been killed in the first days of the war, while leading Tag and his crew behind the Soviet lines, she too had had to deny her grief, turn her sorrow and anger into a fighting fury, and purge herself in battle. She also knew that Tag would not be allowed that luxury. His shoulder was a mess and would keep him out of action for some days or weeks. Her urge to protect and comfort him warred with her realization that what he needed most to sustain him was duty.

"Yes," she said, "but I think I need you to help me make sense of it. I sent all their documents and maps back with them to Colonel Barlow, but I have translations of my debriefings with them. But that is for later. Is the shoulder very bad, Max?"

He rolled his head, looked at her, and cocked a crooked smile. "If it weren't for the honor of the thing, I'd as soon have walked."

The allusion was lost on Giesla, but she recognized her lover's facetious humor, his tough wit, and laughed lightly. "Max," she said, squeezing his hand, "this time I am afraid you will have to ride. As soon as Bones is finished, we are returning to the mineworks. Colonel Barlow is waiting on us."

"Where's Wheels?" Tag said suddenly, trying to crane his neck.

"He is taken care of, Max. Everything is in hand. I want you to ride with me now. That is okay?"

Tag relaxed in the seat and returned the pressure of her hand. "Okay," he said, "okay." His tongue was beginning to slur. "Home, James, home." He closed his eyes and smacked his lips.

Giesla looked at Bones, who was finishing with Tag's first aid.

"Help me sit him up, ma'am," the medic said, "so I can tape this arm down."

When they had finished immobilizing the arm and shoulder, Tag was deadweight. Giesla strapped him in the seat.

"I gave him another pop of morphine," Bones said. "He ought to be out until we get back."

"Thank you," Giesla said. "Please tell Lieutenant Prentice that we are ready."

Giesla led the column herself, followed by the Bradleys, the No Slack Too, and her other two Jagd Kommando vehicles. It was an easy passage, even a pleasant one at any other time. The early autumn crispness was palpable in the air that flowed through the vents in the cowl of the gun vehicle, and the hint of fall colors on the leaves of the oaks put a soft edge on the scenery, but Giesla hardly noticed. She was preoccupied with the man beside her, who still moaned occasionally through the fog of painkillers, and with the things she had not told him.

According to what Colonel Barlow had last told her, the Soviet armies in the north had apparently recovered from the Allied counterattack and showed signs of regaining their poise. The cease-fire was, with minor exceptions, holding, but it looked less and less to the Allies' advantage. The political agreements that had brought it about and had seemed likely to leave room for some sort of negotiated settlement were wearing thin as the Soviets consolidated their gains. True, their armies in Lower Saxony and the Low Countries were overextended and could not possibly hold the ground they had taken, and the First Guards were still trapped, largely thanks to Tag's interdiction of their attempted evacuation, but the rulers in the Kremlin, if not the soldiers in the field, seemed increasingly intractable to quick talks and had once already rejected any discussion of an armistice.

Equally, Ross Kettle was fixated on punishing the Red Army for unleashing nuclear madness on the battlefield, and his dazzling successes had given him a political leverage that public opinion throughout NATO supported. He would not have his hands tied by politics. Giesla could see the war bogging down into an extended battle of attrition, one that would grind her country to dust between the stones of arrogance and vengeance. And in her worst imaginings, she could foresee a Soviet need for battlefield success forcing them into another nuclear venture, this time with strategic weapons, all the way to the end of the world.

Less than three hours later, the raider column had crossed the Danube and were climbing again into the Swabian Jura, toward their redoubt in the abandoned mineworks. Tag was beginning to come around, and once reached out to touch Giesla on the arm, but it was not until they had crested the mountain chain that he spoke.

"Where are we?" he asked thickly. "Is this the Jura?"

Giesla handed him a water bottle and said, "Yes. Here, drink this. You sound like a frog."

He drank and gargled and passed it back to her.

"How is the shoulder now?" Giesla said.

"I think it's gonna hurt like hell when this dope wears off."

"Do you want another shot?"

Tag shook his head. "I want to be conscious at least until I've talked to Barlow. I've got satellite pictures to see, those reports of yours to read. The No Slack Too needs some work, and the . . ."

"Max," Giesla said, cutting off his feverish recital, "let the rest of us pick up the fight for a while."

"I'm not going to any goddamn hospital," Tag said sullenly. "They're not taking me out of the field, and you're not going to let them."

"No, of course not," she lied. "But as you said, wait until you have spoken to Colonel Barlow. We are all still under orders, Max."

Tag fell silent, the pain obviously returning.

The mine and the area around it had undergone vast changes in the short time Tag had been on his mission. A full reinforced battalion of Rangers had invested the position and established a fixed perimeter, complete with razor wire, crew-served weapons emplacements, and sandbagged foxholes. The vehicles and atomic warheads from the Communist convoy that the raiders had ambushed had been cleared, and Barlow had a field kitchen and command center set up in the mine caverns. There was beer and beefsteak for the men of the raider command.

Barlow came himself to help Tag out of the Kommando vehicle and led him into one of the mine shafts, where a dispensary was set up. When Tag was resting comfortably on one of the cots, Barlow poured each of them a large bourbon from a steel flask.

"Compliments of General Kettle, Max," the tall black colonel said, handing Tag the mug of whiskey. Barlow let Tag take a long drink before he said, "I'm sorry about your driver, Max. I've relayed my recommendation to Colonel Menefee that he be put in for the DSC. Do you want me to draft a letter to his family for you?"

"No. Thanks," Tag said, staring into his cup. "He was my friend. It's something I need to do."

Barlow nodded.

"What's our next move, Colonel? I need to get back on that horse."

"I understand, Max, but you're not fit to break up a cat fight right now. Besides, at the moment there's a lot of political heat coming down on the general from your foray, but that's not what you want to hear. We don't have all the assessments in yet, but indications are that the First Guards Army is in total disarray because of your action. So we don't want to press our luck on that front." Barlow took a sip of whiskey. "There are big things afoot, Max, in both the political and the military arenas, and the First Guards are in the middle of both, I'm afraid. Our situation in the north is improving, on the whole, and the Cav has pinched Ivan off at the Fulda Gap. The Soviet line is stalled. Down here, I'm afraid it's something of a standoff between Kettle and the Soviet general staff over who is going to lose face."

Barlow paused. He could see that he was losing Tag's attention to the pain.

"Listen, Max," he said, "all this can wait. I've got a real doctor coming in the morning, so do us both a favor and get yourself a hypo and some sleep. Okay?"

"That an order?" Tag mumbled.

"I can make it one, if that's what it takes."

"Okay," said Tag. "Okay. It's just hard to let up."

"Enjoy it while you can," Barlow said as he stood up. "I'm sure the general will have plans for you by the time that shoulder mends."

Tag was glad for that.